Stegalegs and the Stormflower

For

Benaiah Reuben Joshua Smith

and Sylvia Katharine Lamin

And

in loving memory of my twin-cousin, Louisa

2QT Limited (Publishing)

First Edition published 2019
2QT Limited (Publishing)
Settle, North Yorkshire BD24 9RH
www.2qt.co.uk

Cover design and illustrations by Tom Cockeram©

Printed in UK by Lightning Source (UK) Limited

A CIP catalogue record for this book is available
from the British Library

ISBN 978-1-913071-25-7

Stegalegs and the Stormflower

Reviews

'Armed only with a net, Jilly sets off on a mission to catch an elusive Fogling. But Jilly is not alone. The strange characters in Whey Wood force Jilly to make difficult decisions. "Stegalegs and the Stormflower" introduces the reader to a wonderful, hidden world, painted with vibrant, poetic prose. The reader will cheer Jilly on, sharing her curiosity and willing her to make the right choices.'
W. Rowe: MA Ed, Primary school teacher

'Great alliteration makes reading so much fun.'
R. Perry: Scientist

'I totally loved this story. My imagination took over completely. I can't wait to read it to my young daughter.'
S. Brett: Parent

'A great read!'
S. Hayler: Secondary school teacher

'I read 'Stegalegs at Spinning River' and loved that. 'Stegalegs and the Stormflower' follows on well. It gave me a strong message of perseverance. It was quite funny in parts. The story left me in suspense, especially when Jilly fell into the river. And I love the Foglings! Who knows what strange creatures might be out there in our world?'
Erika Addis: Year 8

'Really good characters. It kept me guessing. The cliffhangers are great!'
L. Hayler Yr 4

Books in the Jilly Jonah series
Stegalegs at Spinning River
Stegalegs and the Stormflower

**Other books for teens/adults by
Katharine Ann Angel**
Being Forgotten
The Froggitt Chain
The Burglar's Baby
Children of the Red Dot . Falling

If you have enjoyed any of the authors books, please leave a review on a social media site or on the online review page of the bookshop where you bought it

Acknowledgements

I am indebted to:
My artist friend, Tom Cockeram for the stunning cover design, and the black and white artwork. (tang.mu.designs@googlemail.com)

My musician friend, John Kenny, for letting me include his poem, '87 Storms.

To all who read Stegalegs and the Stormflower before publication, for the invaluable encouragement, enthusiasm, observations and suggestions, especially Erika Addis, Wendy Rowe, Suzy, Lishka and Emi Hayler, Rowena Perry, Sarah Brett and Andrew Gardner.

To Catherine Cousins and 2QT for your kind advice and encouragement, and making the whole publishing process enjoyable.

A poem about a storm by musician John Kenny

'87 Storms

In the still sleeping night
shaken, awaken
          The world belittled
Lilliput now beneath the shrieking wind
It storms the house, threatens the windows
                         and the curtains tremble
          Striding across the land
Terrorising the hedges and houses and the trees
Oooh, the singing, ringing trees have been through this all before
          Bowing, bending through the aeons
                    They know what to do
                         when the wind comes to roar

Deceptively at first it tickles their leaves
               and strokes their branches
But they are wise and just as old as the wind
          They know to settle their roots down deeply

When the wind gets tired of games
He huffs proud and bellows
          "I am as old as time,
               bold as fire,
                    potent as flood water!"
     Crashing, carousing he sets about to prove it

At the window, in awe of his might and power
I wonder how many continents he strode across
How many seas he whipped up
          and left behind in a rage
               To be in my garden tonight
                    Shouting and howling and playing with the trees

Contents

1
The Fogling Net

Thunder growled over Whey Wood.

Jilly Jonah of Whey House leapt out of bed. 'It's Saturday!' She high fived a cardboard box and knocked it off her desk. She picked it up, hugged it, and whispered, 'I've got a brilliant idea and it can't wait!'

All over the box Jilly had drawn cats and cows, spiders and sunflowers, clouds and lightning, lakes and mountains. She had cut flaps for a door and two windows. Above the door Jilly had scrawled, 'My pet Fogling,' in a fat felt pen.

Jilly pulled her favourite hoodie over a t-shirt and leggings. She glanced at her reflection in the mirror and, forgetting about her baby brother asleep in the next room, she squealed, 'I'm off to catch a Fogling!' She grabbed her trainers and bounced down the creaky stairs. She jumped over the bottom three steps and landed with a thump in the hallway. The baby wailed in his cot.

'Now look what you've done, you've woken Christopher!' called Jilly's mum, Gemma, from behind her laptop in the sitting room, 'Where're you going?'

'Nowhere!'

'Put your coat on!'

'I am. I mean, I will. See you later, Mum!'

'Did you put my silk scarf back in my room like I told you to? I want to wear it to my cousin's wedding next week.'

'I did. I will.'

'Breakfast is in fifteen minutes,' added Gemma, flicking through the news headlines.

Forgetting her coat, Jilly slammed the door behind her and yelled, 'You won't let me have a rabbit or a guinea-pig, so I'm going to get myself a Fogling.'

Jilly ran down the path to the far corner of the garden. Years ago, someone had hammered some planks together and made a shed. One rotten plank hung loose by a single nail. All around the shed huge, dying sunflowers bent their heavy, brown heads.

Jilly pulled the rickety door. *Creeeeak* went the rusty hinges. A mouse scurried down through a hole in the floorboards. A cloud of mosquitos flew out of the shed. One flew up Jilly's nose. 'Atishoo!' she sneezed.

The day the Jonah family moved into Whey House they'd chucked all their junk in the shed and totally forgotten about it. As Jilly scanned the mess, she muttered, 'Bucket and spade, cricket stumps, inflatable dingy, Diabolo, oh, there's the windbreak for the beach.'

Jilly squeezed in among the junk. She rummaged behind plant pots, under the folding garden chairs and inside boxes of crockery. 'Aha!' she cried, spotting two dusty fishing nets jammed between a wonky shelf and a ripped golf bag. One net had a circular head for catching crabs in rockpools. The other had a massive square head. Her dad used it for landing the mackerel he'd caught off the rocks with a rod and line.

'That's a perfect Fogling-catcher!' grinned Jilly. Balancing on a deflated football, she reached for the square net. Just then, a cloud covered the sun. The shed grew dark.

Jilly shuddered, 'What a pain, it looks like rain!' She peered through a cracked window to check for Kerry Muckle. A crane fly had settled on the grubby glass. Jilly told it, 'If Kerry sees me, she'll ask me to help her fetch in the washing.'

Kerry Muckle had no family of her own, so Jilly's mum, Gemma, invited her to live with them. Before that, Kerry had lived in the women's hostel where Gemma worked. Kerry was mostly kind but very bossy. She often warned Jilly, 'Whey Wood is a dangerous place. Don't forget what happened last time you went there. It was terrible. Absolutely terrible.'

'It's just a wood!' retorted Jilly.

'Stop arguing with me. You don't know Skiddley-Diddley-Squat about what is safe and what is not. What if you fell into the stream? Or caught your foot in a rusty old trap? And don't go in that shed either. It's full of sharp saws, lethal lawnmowers and broken tools.'

Jilly thought, 'Kerry can't scare me. I'm in the shed and I'm perfectly fine. Nothing terrible happened.' Jilly breathed on the crane fly. It shuddered a little but stayed on the window.

The sheets on the washing line flapped. There was no sign of Kerry. Jilly stepped out of the shed. A stiff breeze blew her wild red curls over her eyes. She fumbled in her pocket for a bobble but found only her mum's scarlet silk scarf. She wrapped it around her head and knotted it over her forehead. Her hair stuck up like froth on raspberry milkshake.

Jilly wagged her finger at the sunflowers, 'What are you lot staring at?' She whacked their huge dead heads with the net, scattering seeds and insects in all directions. Some seeds fell among the purple thistles, some between the crazy paving, and others landed on hard soil. In a blink, a flock of sparrows appeared. Up-down-up-down-up-down went their little brown heads, peck, peck, peck, devouring every seed they could find.

Jilly asked them, 'Haven't we met before somewhere?' The sparrows hesitated. They cocked their heads, '*You talking to us?*' they seemed to say, then in a flutter they were gone.

Twelve seeds fell onto soft soil and sunk down, tucking themselves in for a long sleep.

One single, solitary seed slipped into the breast pocket of Jilly's hoodie.

The Seed of the Stormflower.

*

Jilly heard the soft crunch of gravel on the driveway of Whey House. 'Dad's pedalling off on his bike to meet his mates. They're cycling twice around the Guild Wheel for Children in Need,' Jilly thought as she watched the electric double gates close behind him. She did a double thumbs-up and grinned, 'Now for my amazing, marvellous, famous Fogling-catcher expedition!'

Jilly ducked under a sickly lime tree. She skipped beyond the sycamore saplings and onto the track that led into Whey Wood.

*

Ting! Ting! Ting!

'Stegalegs? Is that you, Stegalegs?' Jilly hadn't seen him since – well, since the last time she'd been here. *Ting, ting, ting,* sang the bluebells as Stegalegs passed by. Jilly looked high and low, but she could not see her secretive eight-legged friend.

Boom, boom, boom. Jilly pressed her hand over her beating heart and cried, 'Stegalegs, I'll burst if you don't speak to me, I'll explode with excitement, I'll . . .'

Trees rustled. A shadow passed overhead.

'Stegalegs?' Jilly stuttered. Her mouth turned dry, 'Is that you, Stegalegs? Are you standing over me like you did last time?' She looked up and saw - not the eight huge, hairy legs of Stegalegs, but trees rustling in the wind. And the shadow overhead was not the belly of an enormous spider, but simply rain clouds gathering.

'*Ting!*' sang the bowing bluebells. A raindrop fell onto an azure flower-head.

'Oh!' gasped Jilly because it looked stunning. The droplet wobbled on the petal, magnifying the delicate veins of the flower. The raindrop swelled. It slid down, dripped off the petal and landed on the grass.

'Boooom!' growled the woods, but it was not the woods.

'Crack!' snapped a branch, but it was not a branch.

'Help!' cried Jilly. She ducked, but nothing hit her.

'Zig-zag-zig!' Lightning flashed. Its forked tongue stabbed the ground.

'Boooom!' rumbled the thunder.

'Crack, flash, bang!' raged the storm.

'Ji . . lly,' called her mother from far, far away, 'Come in quick, it's going to chuck it down!'

Jilly did not hear Gemma. She wandered further and further into Whey Wood. A few massive raindrops fell but not enough to bother Jilly into running home. 'Plap, plap,' they slapped on Jilly's nose and shoulders. They hit the stream and bounced up.

Jilly tossed her head. 'Who cares about a stupid storm? Got to cross that stream. Got to find Hamelin Lake. Hamelin Lake leads to Spinning River. Spinning River leads to Silk Falls, and Silk Falls is where the Foglings play. I'm going to Silk Falls to catch a Fogling and no one can stop me.'

Jilly slid down the bank beside the stream. Standing as close as she could to the water's edge, Jilly pulled the fishing net back over her shoulder like a javelin and threw it over the water to the other side. Then Jilly leapt over, landing with a skid and a tumble. She clambered up the opposite bank, pulling herself up with tree roots that poked through the mud. After a slippery effort she made it to the top. She wiped her muddy hands on her leggings and looked around.

'Now where's my net?' Jilly scratched her head. She scanned the bank, checking it hadn't fallen back into the stream. She checked the bushes and the entrance to a badger's sett. It was no good. Her brilliant, indispensable, fantastic Fogling net had vanished.

2
The Invisible Cat

Sheet lightning flashed, blinding white across the sky.

'Here it is!' hissed a voice.

'Here's what?' Jilly asked, looking about but seeing only a strange curve of white stones hovering over a low branch.

'Flash! Boom!' raged the storm.

'Never stand under a tree in a storm,' Kerry had warned, but Jilly had ignored her.

Jilly was mesmerised by the white stones that swung from side to side like a moon rocking on its back.

'Now you see it, now you don't,' hissed the voice, louder this time.

Jilly stretched out her hand to the stones, 'I'll just . . .'

'Tut, tut, don't touch what you can't see.'

Jilly jumped back. 'You're soft as a kitten!' She felt shocked because even though she hadn't touched the stones, she had felt

fur.

'Soft as a cat, quiet as a mouse, rotten as a rat that can eat a whole house!' yowled the invisible creature, 'Have you lost something?' And there it was. The square net with the long pole, hanging in the air all by itself.

'Hey,' yelled Jilly, 'you nicked my Fogling-catcher. Give it back, it's mine!'

The net swiped the air. Jilly snatched at it but missed.

'Tell me what a Fogling is and you'll get your net back,' said the strange voice. The net whipped round and caught an Emperor dragonfly. The poor creature buzzed angrily for freedom.

'Don't you even know what a Fogling is? They are babies born early in the morning. They come from all over the world to play in the mist over Spinning River.' Jilly jumped up and tried to grab the handle of the net, but it moved away.

'Bet you've never even seen one,' said the voice.

'I've seen loads! Crisp is a Fogling.'

'Crisp?' The net hovered over Jilly's head.

'He's my baby brother. His real name's Chris. When he's a Fogling he turns grey but he's still my brother.' Jilly jumped but the net dived to the ground.

'And you want to catch one?'

'Yes, I'm getting one for a pet, but they're really speedy. When the mist goes away, they zoom back to their homes.' Jilly tried to stamp on the net, but it shifted sideways, and she missed. The white curve of stones laughed.

'They're not stones they're teeth!' cried Jilly.

With a twiddle and a twist, the net turned over. It opened and the dragonfly flew free. Jilly tried one more snatch at the net. Whoomph! The net vanished.

Jilly stamped, 'I've had enough of this stupid game.'

'But I haven't.'

'Well I have.'

'Haven't.'

'Have.'

'Haven't. And I always win the argument.'

At that exact moment the menacing clouds bashed into each other, spilling a zillion raindrops onto Whey Wood. Jilly's crimson hair dripped down her shoulders. Her soaked hoodie stuck to her back. 'Piddling poodles, I'm drenched!' she cried.

'Help me,' whined the voice.

Jilly was amazed to see a bedraggled, long-haired tabby slumped in a puddle on the path. 'Ha! You're just a silly cat,' Jilly scoffed.

'I'm not silly. Only invisible. And I'm not a cat. You're thinking of the Cheshire cat from another story, but I'm not him, not her, not it. I repeat, I am not a cat.'

'People talk. Cats don't.'

'Exactly. Right at this exact minute I do have cat's teeth and cat's fur and cat's whiskers so call me a cat if you must, but I'm not what or who you think I am. Call me . . . um . . . Barker.'

'Um-Barker? Why the hesitation? Did you just make that name up?'

'Are you calling me a liar? I hope not. Call me plain old Barker.' The cat shook his head, 'Brrrr, look the state of me, soggy as a sandwich at the seaside, sad as a sausage on a barbeque.'

'Why so sad?'

'I'm soaked to the skin meaning I can't stay invisible. What shall I do? I'll never be invisible again if you don't help me.'

'After you stole my net? Get out of that puddle yourself.'

'Then will you dry me?'

'Do I look like I carry a hair-dryer?'

Barker shook his soggy head, 'A bitty-witty towel would do.'

'Here's the deal,' Jilly decided, shaking water from her hair, 'You give me back my net and I'll give you a towel.'

'But you haven't got a towel.'

'Congratulations, you noticed. But you have got my net, so we're evens.' Jilly marched past the cat. She deliberately stomped as hard as she could in the puddle.

'Oy, you big meanie,' groaned Barker. His whiskers drooped into the water, 'Don't you know you reap what you sow? Splash a cat, you watch your back.' Barker slithered out of the puddle and, with his belly scraping over the ground, he skulked under some brambles and into the undergrowth. He growled loudly and, with a furious flick of his tail, he was gone.

'Stop, thief, come back this minute, you've nicked my net!' Jilly tried to crawl after Barker, but it was impossible. She scratched her cheek on a thorn. 'Ouch, that hurt!' she squealed as she reversed out. 'If I ever see that crazy cat again, I'll . . . I'll . . . I'll chuck you in Spinning River so you'll never be invisible again!"

Jilly stood up. She stayed completely still to listen for rustling, but she could not hear Barker in the brambles. 'I'm fed up now,' she yelled, 'so give me back my net!'

Jilly held her breath and waited for Barker's reply.

Nothing.

*

In a deep, dark corner of her pocket, the dampness of the rain softened the hard shell of the solitary sunflower seed.

3
Chuzzle and the Quiet Cow

The morning sun warmed the glistening trees. Raindrops dripped from their leaves like jewels into puddles below. Jilly stamped on the reflection of the sun. The sparkling water splashed her leggings. She punched the sky and shouted, 'Who cares what Kerry thinks? I'm not scared of any storm! And I don't need a stupid net to catch a Fogling. I'll catch one of those grey beastie babies with my own bare hands.'

Jilly stared at her hands. She imagined snatching a Fogling as it frolicked in the mist. She pretended to squeeze it against her hoodie, knowing that if she let go it would whizz home to its family. 'Hello, little Fogling. Where in the world did you come from?' she said, pretending to stroke it, 'I've got a lovely cardboard box for you to live in.'

Jilly came upon a sprawling mulberry bush covered in crimson berries. She ambled around it and stopped abruptly. There stood a black-and-white cow with its head down, ripping up the long grass, chewing slowly. When she raised her head, frothy green slather dripped from the corners of her mouth right down to the ground.

'What're you doing in Whey Wood?' asked Jilly, not expecting an answer because this was, after all, a cow.

The cow lowered her head and tore up another mouthful of grass. Crunch, crunch, crunch, it munched. 'Hey, Mrs Moo, budge over - you're in my way,' commanded Jilly, but the cow only turned her head and continued to chew and slather, chew and slather, chew and slather.

'Be like that!' Jilly ducked down and dived under the cow, bumping the back of her head against its soft tummy. She stumbled out on the other side, then fell headlong into a cowpat. Dung-flies flew in all directions but quickly return to their stinky feast. Jilly scrambled to her feet. Her hoodie was covered in dung.

'I pong and it's all your fault,' she said. The cow blinked her long eyelashes, lowered her head, and chewed and slathered and chewed again.

'Don't you even care?' Jilly cried, throwing open her arms.

The cow raised her head and snorted loudly. Frothy, green slather shot out of her nose.

'Oh yuk!' cried Jilly. She turned her back on the cow and ran. A slab of dung clung fast to the front of her hoodie. After a while, Jilly stopped to catch her breath. 'Why am I running? It's only a cow,' she panted. She had a quiet word with herself, 'Slow down, Jilly. Calm down. Breathe slowly. And don't forget the Foglings.'

Jilly set off again, then stopped sharp. Her hand flew to her mouth. 'Oh, you gave me a fright,' she said to a short, bow-legged man with curly green hair and piercing, azure eyes. His face, wrinkled from living in the open air, cracked into a huge grin. In his gnarled hands he held a length of tatty rope that trailed over the ground.

'Nice to meet you again. Have you seen Nasuto?' he asked.

Jilly didn't answer because she didn't recognise the man, even though he'd said, 'Nice to meet you again,' as if they'd met before.

The man stepped back, 'Don't be alarmed. I mean you no harm. The name's Chuzzle. Chuzzle, the famous Green Prince of Whey Wood. Look at my lovely hair. That's algae, that is. Caused by too much sun, too much rain and sleeping outside in the dirt. Sun, rain, dirt. Never wash. Altogether they make algae. Mucky stuff, but I'm proud of it.'

Still Jilly said nothing but knitted her eyebrows together in a puzzled expression.

'I asked you about Nasuto?' Chuzzle opened both hands and raised his eyebrows.

Jilly echoed, 'Nasuto?'

'My cow. I only bought her yesterday and already lost. A real beauty. Cost me five beans. A fair deal, I'd say.'

'Beans?' Jilly repeated. Kerry Muckle would tick her off for asking so many questions. She'd tap the side of her nose, and say, 'Nosy, nosy, leave the poor man alone. Curiosity killed the cat!' but Jilly couldn't help herself. Two things were her thing, science books and questions, and Jilly loved asking questions. Once she started it was difficult to stop.

'Five beans for a fine cow,' sighed Chuzzle.

'Is that all? Where did you get it? Can I buy one? I'll nip home for five beans. What if I got ten beans? Could I buy two? Or twenty beans? How many for a hundred beans?' Jilly could tell Chuzzle wasn't interested selling her a cow or anything else, so she said, 'If you really want to know, I did see your cow back there. What's her name again?'

'Nasuto, after the famous dinosaur Nasutoceratops Titusi.'

'Hmm, I see,' said Jilly, not understanding at all.

'I doubt you see. I doubt that very much,' said Chuzzle.

'Nas-Suit-Oh-Sarah-Tops Tea-Too-See,' repeated Jilly carefully, 'Wow, cool name!'

'Nasuto is enough for a cow. And you say you've seen her? Hmm. As I said, I doubt that very much.' Chuzzle shook his head and tutted.

Jilly stamped her foot to prove how truthful she was being. 'Black, white, big eyes, eats grass, won't budge.'

Chuzzle stuck out his bottom lip and shrugged, 'Which describes any-old-body's cow. Nasuto is a very particular cow. She is me - I mean, she is my cow.' Chuzzle dropped his rope on the ground and changed the subject, 'Hey, can you whistle?' He put two fingers from each hand into his mouth, pulled them back and blew very hard.

'Ouch!' Jilly covered her ears with her hands.

'Your turn,' chuckled Chuzzle. Jilly stuck her fingers into her mouth and blew a loud raspberry full of spit. She wiped her fingers on her hoodie.

'No, not like that - like this . . .' Chuzzle whistled again. He scared three tatty crows out of a tatty tree, caw, caw, caw! A black feather fluttered down to Jilly's feet, but she ignored it. The whistling thing was too wonderful to be bothered with a feather. She tried again and managed a spitty 'Eeeek.'

'Good, good. A small sound is better than no sound,' Chuzzle nodded his approval. Jilly gave it another go. She blew as hard as she could. Her whistle was so shrill Chuzzle punched the air.

'Griddling greatnesses, you've got it! Brilliant. Okay, so when you see my cow, give that exact same whistle and I'll be there.' He blinked his electric blue eyes, shook his green hair and did a cartwheel into the bushes.

'Wait, Mr Green Prince, you forgot your rope!' Jilly shouted. She picked up the scraggy rope and waved it. The bushes rustled, then all was still. Just like Barker, Chuzzle had vanished in the undergrowth. 'Best look after this rope in case I see him again,' Jilly said. She knotted the rope around her waist and set off walking once more, telling herself over and over again, 'Forget cats. Forget cows. Forget Chuzzle. Focus on Foglings.'

Here the path narrowed. Branches brushed Jilly's hair, forcing her to dip lower and lower until she was crawling through a tunnel of twigs and leaves where only badgers go. It was almost impossible to see the way ahead. Thorns scratched her face, and stones stabbed her hands and knees. Jilly lay flat and wriggled forward like a snake, thinking, 'What if it's a dead end and I can't turn back?'

Wriggling was exhausting work. Jilly rested. To calm herself, she laid her cheek flat on the warm earth. A red ladybird with seven black spots stumbled past her nose, around her forehead and out of sight. Jilly lifted her head wondering where it had gone. Beyond her, giant tree roots arched out of the earth, stretching and twisting. Between the root arches Jilly reckoned she saw diamonds sparkling, blue and white, dark and light. 'What are those?' she asked. She crept towards them. She squeezed under a tree root and popped up the other side. Jilly burst into the light and jumped up.

'Sparkling water,' Jilly cried, flinging her arms wide, 'This is Lake Hamelin where I swam before. This is where I canoed with my friends.' Steam swirled and curled over the surface of the water. 'Foglings love this sort of thing!' Jilly ran down to the water's edge. Some fussy ducks flapped and quacked in alarm.

'Don't be daft,' laughed Jilly, 'it's only me, Jilly Jonah.' The ducks flew away and all was quiet.

Too quiet.

Shhh.

*

A tiny blob of dung fell off Jilly's hoodie and landed in her pocket. It covered the solitary seed.

4
Jackal-Yackle Snickle-Snackle

Crack! A sound like lightning but not lightning.

'Snap!' Jilly swung round just in time to see a massive branch break off a tree trunk and crash to the ground. Twigs broke, leaves fluttered, and a squirrel scarpered as the branch smashed into the earth. A long, white scar split the tree trunk where the branch had ripped off.

'Aargh!'

Someone had fallen.

'You okay?' Jilly called. Seconds before she'd been standing precisely where the branch had landed. She shuddered, 'If I hadn't rushed to see the lake I'd have been squished.'

Two small hands appeared over the fallen branch. A cheerful boy with a grubby face and wavy hair tied in a ponytail, heaved himself up onto it with an almighty "Oomph!" The branch bounced as the boy balanced on it. He wore a checked jacket with fringed seams hanging from the waist and sleeves. His trousers were torn and baggy. His holey shoes were tied onto his feet with string. On his back the boy carried a frayed, patchwork knapsack.

'Da-dah!' he chimed, standing on tiptoes and lifting his hands as if he'd won a tennis trophy.

'Da-dah?' Jilly mocked, 'Da-dah? You could have been killed and all you can say is da-dah? Why are you showing off?'

The boy marched up to Jilly. He held out his hand and grinned, 'How do you do. I'm Jackal-Yackle Snickle-Snackle, first of The Nine.'

Jilly didn't want to shake hands, but neither did she want to be rude, so she stuck out her hand and said, 'I'm Jilly Jonah. It's a good thing Kerry Muckle didn't see. She'd have warned you about being killed.'

'Yup, that's the problem with climbing, the higher you go the further you fall. But I love climbing. I simply love it.'

'Can't see the point myself – except for escaping predators.'

'Then you've never been on top of the world and seen east and west at the same time, or spied on people so far below they look like ants, or . . .'

'Oh, but I have,' said Jilly, remembering how she'd once fled from an aggressive badger defending her young. She'd had to climb the highest tree in Whey Wood where she'd perched on a branch, marvelling at the view over the treetops, 'But then I fell and . . .' Jilly began to tell her story, but the boy wasn't listening.

'Apple or beans?' Jackal-Yackle Snickle-Snackle dipped his hands into his trouser pockets and pulled out five purple-speckled kidney beans and two crab apples.

'Defo not beans,' laughed Jilly. She took an apple, 'Thanks.'

Jackal-Yackle Snickle-Snackle munched on a bean, pulled a face, then spat it out all over Jilly's hoodie, 'Ugh, that needs cooking!'

'And that's disgusting!' said Jilly, flicking soggy lumps off her clothes. She thought for a moment, then asked, 'Where did you get those beans from?'

'Here and there,' smiled the boy, 'here and there. They grow on beanstalks, don't you know?'

'So you never sold a cow to a man with green hair?'

'Me sell a cow? I've lived in Whey Wood for centuries and I've never even seen a real live cow.' Jackal-Yackle Snickle-Snackle bit into the second apple, 'Mmm, yummy. Come on, Jilly Jonah, come with me,' he beckoned, 'I want to show you something amazing.'

Jilly ran as fast as she could alongside the lake, but it was impossible to keep up with the boy. He was so light on his feet. It was as if his he had springs for ankles. His ill-fitting shoes didn't slow him down one bit.

'Wait for me, I've got a stitch,' Jilly panted. She bent over, clutching her sides. By the time the pain had subsided, Jackal-

Yackle Snickle-Snackle had leapt and bounced away until he was only a springing dot in the distance.

*

Jilly plonked herself down on a large flat rock. 'Who cares about the amazing thing he talked about? I've got my own plans.' She finished her apple and tossed the core into the lake. It bobbed merrily downstream.

As Jilly stared at the core, she heard a low whisper, 'Follow Jackal-Yackle Snickle-Snackle.'

Jilly looked around, 'Who said that? Where are you?'

The voice came from a clump of bulrushes poking out from the shallows. On top of each bulrush was a fuzzy, brown brush-head. The bulrushes rustled although there was no breeze. Jilly shuddered. Above her, the pale blue blanket of sky packed away the last of the day's storm clouds.

A whisper; 'Follow Jackal-Yackle Snickle-Snackle.'

'Stega . . . Stegalegs?' Jilly felt a teeny bit scared. She stood up and peered into the bulrushes. A hammock of spidery web splattered with flies hung between the stalks. 'That's his favourite food,' smiled Jilly, remembering the time her enormous eight-legged friend had (so kindly) offered her a snack of scrummy flies, 'Now I know you're hiding somewhere!'

No reply.

'Just so you know, I don't care about Jacky-Yacky Snicky-Snacky what's-his-name. I've only come to catch a Fogling. Please, Stegalegs, help me find a Fogling.' If anyone could help, Jilly knew that Stegalegs could.

A dazzle of damselflies flickered just above the surface of the water. 'Oh,' gasped Jilly, marvelling at their shimmering, sapphire beauty. Overhead, an eagle spread its shining wings against the sky. Jilly looked up, straight into its dark, searching eyes, before the eagle soared up and away over the clifftop.

'Stegalegs, Stegalegs, help, help, help,' Jilly chanted, but Stegalegs stayed silent. 'Have it your own way. Fine, I'll follow that boy then. But if I do what you want, you'd better find me a Fogling to catch or I'll be mega mad.' Jilly set off after Jackal-Yackle Snickle-Snackle, all the time wondering what could possibly be so amazing.

5
The Song of Courage

Jilly's tummy rumbled. She groaned, 'That apple didn't exactly fill me up. I wish I'd brought a cheese sandwich.'

'Here y'are!' The boy sprung in front of Jilly and offered her a carrot.

'You again,' Jilly said, 'but you were so far ahead of me. How did you get here so fast?'

'Far, near, everywhere is here,' said Jackal-Yackle Snickle-Snackle, and gave her the carrot.

'Thanks,' Jilly said, and bit into it, 'I usually peel carrots, but this is scrummy with the skin on.' She took a second bite.

'When you're properly hungry everything is yummy. Here, try this.'

'Celery? No thanks.'

'That's because you've already got a carrot.' Jackal-Yackle Snickle-Snackle bit into his celery with a loud crunch. He talked with his mouth full, 'Can you walk a bit faster? We're going to be late for The Amazing with a capital A.'

'The Amazing what?'

'So many questions, so few answers. Tell you what, let's swap shoes.'

'My smart trainers for your stringy old rubbish? No way.'

'That explains it,' grinned Jackal-Yackle Snickle-Snackle.

'Explains what?'

'Why you don't want to help me.'

'You never said you wanted help.'

'Didn't I?' The boy began to run and jump, heading for the magnificent curved waterfalls that fell in curtains over so many caves.

'I don't get it. He never explains what he means,' Jilly

mumbled to herself as the boy leapt from tree to rock like a flea on a dog. Jilly chomped on her carrot as she walked on, muttering, 'I like my trainers, and I'm keeping them.'

Jilly scanned Spinning River for Foglings, but there were none hanging about. Deep down she knew she wouldn't find one yet. Foglings only appear early in the morning when the rising sun warms the rivers and lakes, evaporating the water into a swirling mist. The chubby, grey babies love to tumble on the mist, fluttering all over the place like blossom in a breeze. Still Jilly searched high and low, and by the time she reached the waterfalls, Jackal-Yackle Snickle-Snackle was nowhere to be seen.

'I did as I was told. I followed the boy, so it's not my fault I lost him,' she said into the air, hoping that Stegalegs might hear her.

*

The noise of the waterfalls deafened Jilly. Water gushed down the mountains, crashing over the cliffs, thundering into the lake, throwing up froth, and forming whirlpools between the rocks. Over the racket, Jilly heard a high-pitched, piercing cry of the eagle as it searched for food. From her previous expedition Jilly remembered where its eerie was, a mess of sticks and bones, high on a ledge.

Jilly followed Piper's Path that wound behind the waterfalls. A wall of water separated her from the lake. It thrilled her to peer through the falling water, seeing how it caught the light, creating rainbows and diamond splashes. She passed the cave where she'd once rescued a lost boy called Marcus.

'Did I hear laughter,' Jilly asked herself, 'or is that the sound of water hitting the rocks?' Jilly walked around the headland. To her right, the cliff rose sharply, and to her left lay the lake. Jilly followed the footprints of people and animals in the mud until she was forced to stop because Piper's Path dipped downhill and this part was flooded. Since the heavy rain, Hamelin Lake had overflowed into the dip. Jilly looked around for a stick and found one. She poked the flood to find the ground beneath the water.

'Not too deep,' Jilly decided, 'it should be easy enough to walk through.' She removed her trainers, tied the laces together and hung them around her neck. She took off her socks and stuffed them into the large pocket along the front of her hoodie. She shoved her leggings up to her knees, then dipped her toes into the water.

'Argh, that's freezing,' Jilly giggled, 'but I can't go back or I won't get to Silk Falls in time to catch a Fogling.' She stepped into the water. It tickled her ankles. Another step. The water lapped around her knees. Another, and she was up to her thighs. Jilly's leggings were sopping wet, but they'd dry soon enough. She placed one hand on a rock at the base of the cliff to steady herself and . . . whoops, she slipped into Spinning River.

'Help!' screamed Jilly as the current swept her downstream. She somersaulted over and over in the rapids. She gasped for air, caught sight of the eagle, saw bubbles, couldn't breathe, surfaced and gasped again. Water filled her ears and nose. 'Stegalegs!'

Somewhere above Jilly's head came a quiet voice; 'Your shoes.'

'Shoes? Do you mean my trainers?' Jilly wanted to say, but her mouth was underwater so she couldn't speak. *Shoes, trainers, shoes, trainers. Do you mean trainers?* Faster and faster, over and over, Jilly tumbled. The water roared over her head and bubbled in her ears.

'Take off your shoes.' The water roared, yet the quiet words sounded clear as a bell.

Jilly wriggled her toes, 'But I'm barefoot!' She lurched forward on another wave and tumbled over. Each time Jilly saw the sky she gasped for a breath. 'I'm being strangled!' she thought, 'My trainers around my neck are full of water - so heavy – so heavy!' She pulled at the laces. Another glimpse of sky. Another breath. Over and over. Jilly wrestled with her trainers. 'Too heavy!' Jilly wrestled the laces, tucked her chin down, pulled the trainers free, and let go. The trainers, still tied together, bounced away over the rapids.

With the weight of water gone, Jilly stopped struggling. Her body floated more easily. She managed a few strong breaststrokes and pulled herself into calmer water. Her arms shook with effort as she aimed for riverbank. Her feet touched down on slimy mud, bumpy pebbles, more slippery mud, and more painfully lumpy pebbles. Jilly slipped and stumbled onto dry land. Her legs felt like jelly. She could hardly stand. She flopped to the ground to catch her breath and lay back panting, feeling the warm sunshine on her face, and being thankful.

*

The sound of chitter-chattering woke Jilly. She opened her eyes. Shadows passed over the blue sky.

Someone shouted, 'Hey, you lot, she's awake! That girl's woken up.'

Jilly sat bolt upright. The sun sparkled like rubies in her dripping hair. She leaned forward and coughed up water. Her face juddered and her teeth chattered. Her body shook from shock and wouldn't stop shaking.

'Blanket!' someone cried. A shabby, grey blanket was thrown over Jilly's shoulders. A girl with ebony hair rubbed Jilly's back. Jilly's fingers and toes tingled as the blood returned to them.

'Sip of Life!' said a young man, holding a tin mug to Jilly's lips. Steam rose from a sweet, spicy drink. Now her nose was tingling. Jilly took a sip. So good. So warm.

'Song of Courage!' cried a girl, and she began to hum the first line of "If you're happy and you know it clap your hands." Then she burst into a long, 'Ohhhhhh . . .' and everyone joined in,

> *'You don't know what you're doing here yet*
> *You cannot catch a Fogling in a net*
> *But you carry all we need*
> *In a dark and tiny seed*
> *To take us to the Land of Skiddleyphet.'*

Jilly stopped shivering. She looked up, relieved to see a familiar face. 'Jackal-Yackle!' she cried.

'Don't forget the Snickle-Snackle!' he grinned. He swept his arm round, 'Welcome to my family. We are The Nine.'

'The Nine?' Jilly pulled her best 'I'm fascinated and impressed' face.

'We are The Nine who stayed behind after the destruction of the First Beanstalk.'

'Shh,' warned a blue-haired girl, 'you trust too soon. Don't tell her the whole story.'

'Don't worry, I won't,' grinned Jackal-Yackle Snickle-Snackle. Turning to Jilly Jonah he said, 'This is Mr. Jurado.'

'Hi-ho,' grinned an ancient man. His white eyes twinkled behind wire-rimmed circular spectacles and his wispy, white beard wafted softly in the breeze.

'He may be almost blind, but he knows your heart and mind,' explained Jackal-Yackle Snickle-Snackle.

'Is *that* the amazing thing?' coughed Jilly, then she couldn't stop coughing. The dark-haired girl slapped Jilly hard on her back. Jilly spat out some river water.

'Better?' asked the ebony-haired girl. Jilly nodded, but she felt sick.

'It is not a thing,' said Jackal-Yackle Snickle-Snackle placing his hand on the shoulder of one of two girls, both taller than Jilly Jonah. 'Lay down your treasures, sisters. And come here my brothers. Let us greet our new friend.' Nine knapsacks strung with tin mugs, tools, brushes, and other paraphernalia were tossed in a pile.

'Meet my older sister, Zoa, who kindly rubbed your back.' Jackal-Yackle Snickle-Snackle paused to allow the two girls to acknowledge each other. 'And here you have the splendiferous fire-brothers, Minto and Shtomp. Shtomp's the oldest. He wears sunglasses 'cos his eyes are sensitive to light.'

'Fire-brothers?'

'See those scars on their hands and faces? They were toddlers when fire raged through their home-forest. Zoa heard their cries and called me. I can only be in one place at a time, but I move fast. I snatched them from the burning, one infant under each arm, and I brought them here to live with our handsome tribe.'

'Is *that* the amazing thing?' Jilly asked, blinking back tears.

'It is not a thing.'

Mr Jurado said, 'This is Archer.' A lanky boy with a missing tooth gave Jilly a shy nod and a thumbs-up. 'Archer hunts with bow and arrow. Always misses. No harm done. And here we have Joiner, a splendid lad who talks with his hands and his mouth at the same time.'

'Hi-ho, high five,' said Joiner, holding his hand up to Jilly's. His hand was twice the size of hers. It had been scratched by thorns from foraging for food.

'Joiner fixes wood together. Cuts grooves that fit. Anything you ask, he'll build it. Chair. Table. Canoe. Bridge. You name it. And that there's Lumber. He, too, hates attention,' added Mr Jurado. Lumber blushed red, so Jilly blushed too. He was so shy Jilly didn't dare speak to him, but she noticed that his trousers were too long for him.

'We're triplets,' added Joiner, 'all born on the same day.'

'But not real triplets,' laughed Archer, 'because we're from different families.'

'I'm confused,' said Jilly.

'True, they share a birthday, but it's just a coincidence,' said Mr Jurado.

'A very big one,' said Jilly, puffing out her cheeks in amazement.

'And this is Felicity-Blue . . .' The blue-haired girl glared at Jilly. 'Don't be jealous, Felicity-Blue,' warned Mr Jurado.

'Hi, Felicity-Blue.' Jilly returned the taller girl's glare. Felicity-Blue narrowed her eyes and the hairs on the back of Jilly's neck rose. Without blinking, she stared hard at Felicity-Blue while she finished her drink.

'Home time,' said Jilly, handing the tin mug up to Archer. Pulling the grey blanket tight beneath her chin, Jilly struggled to her feet. 'Thanks. That was, um, delicious,' she added, clearing her throat with a polite cough, 'And very nice to meet you. I gotta go.'

'Whoa!' cried Mr. Jurado, holding up his hand like a traffic policeman, 'What about our song?'

'What about it?' Jilly asked.

'The Song of Courage is more than just a song. It is a calling. And you have been called.'

'Really?' said Jilly, rolling her eyes, 'By who? For what?'

'Called by The Nine to give up your own dream for the sake of others.'

'I don't get it.'

'You came to do the impossible, but you are called to do the incredible.'

Jilly giggled, 'That's kind of you to say so, but I don't want a calling, thank-you very much. I'm the sort of person who does her own thing. I came to catch a Fogling for a pet, but things have got in my way. First some stupid invisible cat stole my net, then I . . .'

'Even *with* a net, no one can ever catch a Fogling,' interrupted Mr Jurado holding both hands out towards Jilly, 'Your dream is impossible. Let go, my child. Do a new thing.' A murmur of agreement rumbled round the group.

'Not even Stegalegs can catch a Fogling,' added Zoa, her eyes bright with excitement. Everyone gasped. Lumber slapped his hand over his face to hide his blushes.

'Hush, Zoa,' warned Jackal-Yackle Snickle-Snackle, 'You must never speak that name without good reason.'

Jilly blurted, 'Stegalegs? You've heard of Stegalegs? I call his name all the time and nothing bad ever happens. In fact, most of the time *nothing* happens. If you want another fact, Stegalegs is my friend.'

Again, everyone gasped. Then they all spoke at once.

'Your friend?'

'How is that possible?'

'You've actually met him?'

'What does he look like?'

'Can he talk? What did he say?'

'We've heard of him, but we didn't believe he existed. Tell us, tell us!'

Jilly covered her ears. She hated being the centre of attention at school and she didn't like it any better in Whey Wood.

'Enough!' cried Jackal-Yackle Snickle-Snackle. He fell to his knees, 'Jilly Jonah, you have a calling. You are called to help us climb into the land of . . .'

'Stegalegs?' interrupted Jilly, because she wasn't afraid of the name.

Everyone crowded in, eager to overhear the whole conversation. With a flick of his hand, Jackal-Yackle Snickle-Snackle shooed them away. They took one step back.

Jilly spoke even more loudly, 'I don't have the foggiest where Stegalegs lives. You could check out the bulrushes, or the brambles. I bet he hasn't even got a land. And even if he does, how am I supposed to know the way?'

'I know the way,' said Jackal-Yackle Snickle-Snackle, bowing his head, 'but Jilly Jonah, it is you who carry the Seed of the Stormflower. Without the Stormflower we can never go home.'

Jilly shook her head, but Mr Jurado nodded. Their eyes met. Jilly knew he knew what would happen next.

'I . . . I can't possibly follow you,' Jilly wriggled her toes and saw a brilliant excuse, 'because I've got bare feet! Look, see, I lost my trainers in the river. They were too heavy. Full of water. I had to chuck them away.' Jilly struggled to her feet, but Jackal-Yackle Snickle Snackle stayed on his knees.

'Help me up,' he pleaded.

Jilly reached out and with both hands she pulled him to his feet. Then she noticed that the boy also had bare feet, 'Hey, you've taken off your shoes.'

'For you.'

Jilly pulled a disgusted face, 'No way they'll fit me.' She almost blurted out that they stank and that the soles were holey and the string was tatty, but somehow Jilly managed to keep her mouth shut.

'Try them,' implored the boy.

Jilly shrugged, 'Okay, okay, just for you. I'll try, but I won't buy!' With her mouth downturned because she really did not want to do this, she dipped one big toe into the first ragged shoe. Then her whole foot. It wasn't as bad as she'd feared. In fact, the shoes felt extraordinarily comfortable. She'd never walked in someone else's shoes before. 'You win – for now,' she sighed, slipping on the second shoe, 'but what about you? You'll hurt your own feet on those stones.'

'So be it. Here, let me fix them on for you.' Jackal-Yackle Snickle-Snackle knotted the ragged strings around Jilly's feet. And as the boy worked, Jilly knew she would go with him. She would follow the call of The Nine, Fogling or no Fogling.

If she had known how terrifying the next few hours were going to be, she'd have run home barefoot through thistles and swamps and never, ever returned to Whey Wood.

*

The sun bore down, warming Jilly's breast pocket. Inside, unseen, the seed twitched. It cracked open. A tiny, green shoot poked out.

6
Chinese Whispers

'Follow the boy,' rasped Stegalegs.

Jilly looked at each of The Nine. 'Did you hear that?' she asked.

Mr Jurado nodded his head ever so slightly, but he said nothing. Jilly thought he must have heard Stegalegs just as she had. She remembered what Jackal-Yackle Snickle-Snackle had said about Mr Jurado, 'He may be almost blind, but he knows your heart and mind.'

'Hear what?' said Felicity-Blue, still looking angry for no obvious reason.

'Nothing,' Jilly shrugged. She set off along the stony path with Jackal-Yackle Snickle-Snackle hobbling along beside her.

Zoa called after them, 'Is this it, my brother? Are we going to Skiddleyphet at last?' The others looked hopefully at one another. They'd never known the boy to be so serious.

Jackal-Yackle Snickle-Snackle turned to face Zoa, 'Mr Jurado taught us that the Stormflower will be stronger than the First Beanstalk because there will be not one stalk, but three. Together we will climb to Skiddleyphet, the old with the young, the weak with the strong, the lame with the fleet of foot, the timid with the brave.'

'What do you mean, not one but three?' asked Minto.

'The First Beanstalk was strong, but strength alone is not enough,' said Jackal-Yackle Snickle-Snackle.

'The three are strength, faithfulness and, most powerful of all, selflessness,' said Mr Jurado.

'That means putting others before yourself,' added Zoa, 'which we really do try to do, but it is hard.'

'I'm afraid of the storm to come,' shuddered Felicity-

Blue.

'Me too,' echoed Lumber, patting Felicity-Blue on the shoulder.

'Don't touch me!' Felicity-Blue spat.

Lumber jumped back, 'Oops, soz, my bad!'

'Jilly Jonah's not afraid,' said Joiner, shaking both fists in admiration.

Jilly stopped walking, and everyone stopped with her. Jilly frowned, '*Should I be afraid?*'

Mr Jurado looked at Jilly. He nodded wisely because he knew her thoughts. He said, 'It is better not to know the future, whether it be good or bad.' Six sparrows fluttered by, twittering loudly. 'Look at those birds. Do they worry about tomorrow? Not at all. Today they have food - and life!'

'Birds don't worry, nor do flowers,' said Archer.

Jilly asked, 'Exactly. So why are we worrying? I can't see any storm. Come on, let's get this over with.' Jilly set off again and everybody set off with her. Jilly marvelled at Jackal-Yackle Snickle-Snackle's terrible shoes because they felt as strong as trainers and as comfortable as slippers.

After a while, Jackal-Yackle Snickle-Snackle asked, 'I can tell you want to dance.'

'You can tell nothing. I don't dance,' retorted Jilly. She didn't want to be so grumpy, but she couldn't help it. Acting angry was the only way to stop herself from dancing, but her feet felt so light . . .

'Surely you can't help it!' said Jackal-Yackle Snickle-Snackle and he did a little jig. 'Ouch, ouch, ouch!' he cried as his feet hit the stony path.

'Don't do that,' said Jilly, 'if it hurts.'

'Look behind you, my friend. What do you see?'

'A bunch of miserable looking so-and-sos trailing too far behind us.'

'Why are they miserable?'

'Why are you asking me if you know all the answers?'

'Because if you understood how sad they feel, you'd dance.'

'That makes no sense,' said Jilly. She walked on, shoulder to shoulder with the boy. His ponytail swung and the fringes on his jacket swooshed as he moved. After some time, Jilly added, 'I think it's cruel to dance when others are sad.'

'Dancing gives hope to the down-hearted,' explained Jackal-Yackle Snickle-Snackle. 'Try it. You'll see.'

'But I don't know any steps,' said Jilly.

'I'm not talking about a waltz or a tango or a jive. You've got to learn special steps to do those kind of dances. I'm talking about a different dance, the sort that bubbles up from deep inside you. Joy is a dance from deep inside your heart, Jilly Jonah.'

Jilly shook her head, 'Stop going on about dancing. I don't do joy. You're asking the wrong person. I'm not the dancing type.'

Jackal-Yackle Snickle-Snackle spun round, grinned and waved at the others. He did a little jig, leaping up and clicking his fingers. Archer quickly waved back. Joiner slapped Lumber on the back and together they picked up the pace, with Lumber half-tripping over the bottoms of his trousers. Minto and Shtomp set off marching and singing, "Oh, The Grand Old Duke of York." Felicity-Blue skipped to catch up with Zoa and the two girls chattered cheerfully.

'See what I did?' Jackal-Yackle Snickle-Snackle asked Jilly.

Jilly shook her head, 'Nope.'

'Cheered them up. Even if my feet hurt, I chose to dance in my heart, and they were uplifted.'

Jilly glanced back, 'Mr Jurado has fallen far behind us. We'd better wait for him.'

'Glad you noticed. Very kind of you, but you never need to worry about our grandfather. He guards our back in case of a Chuzzle attack.'

'Chuzzle? Green hair, blue eyes? Lost cow? I met him. Friendly sort of a guy.' Jilly ran her hands over the rope that she'd tied about her waist.

Jackal-Yackle Snickle-Snackle lowered his voice, 'Beware the Chuzzle. He is our only enemy. Since before time began, Chuzzle desired to rule the peaceful land of Skiddleyphet, but he has never entered it. He tried hard enough when the First Beanstalk sprouted. He got scarily close. The Beanstalk shot up, higher than an eagle above the clouds. Chuzzle rushed at it. He pushed past us. He climbed it so quickly . . .'

'Who stopped him?'

'We did.'

'Who's we?'

'Me, everyone's grandfather Mr Jurado, my big sister Zoa, my friend Felicity-Blue, the fire-brothers Minto and Shtomp, and the triplets who are not triplets, Archer, Joiner and Lumber,' Jackal-Yackle Snickle-Snackle explained, 'We were forced to cut the First Beanstalk above us. Straightaway it died and fell to the ground with Chuzzle still clinging on. We all fell to the ground.'

'Ouch! That sounds painful. I once read a story about a boy called Jack who chopped down a beanstalk so the evil giant couldn't follow him.'

'Is that what they say? I'm afraid you've heard Chinese whispers.'

'Chinese whispers?'

'It's when a story is told but never written down. Over many years the story is passed down by word of mouth from generation to generation. Each time it is told, the story changes a tiny bit. By the time you hear the story, it is nothing like the truth. But I know the true story. Shall I tell you?'

'Yes.'

'I, Jackal-Yackle Snickle-Snackle climbed the First Beanstalk ahead of my sister Zoa, and the rest. Lumber shouted, "Watch out below!" Chuzzle was following us. He chased us so fast. He climbed over Lumber and stood on his head, almost kicking him off the beanstalk. Further up the stalk, Chuzzle did the same with Joiner. Many had climbed before us and entered the Gleaming Gate into Skiddleyphet. Chuzzle would not have caught up with us, but we'd been seriously slowed down because the weak, the old and sick could not climb. Hundreds of them crowded at the foot of the First Beanstalk. Before Chuzzle turned up, we Nine did our best to give them piggybacks but it was too hard. We were weak. We gave up. We lost hope.'

'You should never give up.'

'But we did.'

'What happened next?'

'A wonderful thing. Strange silver hammocks appeared on ropes of steel. They came down from the sky, from somewhere above the clouds. We loaded the hammocks with the old and sick, then watched each one being lifted to safety. When the last person had been taken, we began to climb.'

'What about Mr Jurado, he's old. Why didn't he go up in a hammock?'

'Old doesn't always mean weak. He is strong in body, mind and spirit.'

'So, you were all climbing.'

'Yes, but we noticed that the First Beanstalk was shrivelling. Time was running out. 'Hurry!' I cried. But Chuzzle appeared. He's as fit. He's as fast as I am. Faster maybe. He can move like forked lightning. We knew if Chuzzle reached the gates before us he'd go into Skiddleyphet. He'd slam the gates in our faces. We thought . . .' gulped Jackal-Yackle Snickle-Snackle, 'we thought Stegalegs lived in Skiddleyphet. And we believed Chuzzle would kill Stegalegs!'

'You said - you said Stegalegs.'

'Did I?' A tear trickled down the boy's face.

'You said Stegalegs two times. I told you, it's all right. You don't have to be scared of him. I say his name all the time.'

'Yes, I said Stegalegs. And without Stegalegs, Skiddleyphet would be a terrible place.'

'But Stegalegs hangs out in Whey Wood. He can't be in two places at once.'

'Far, near, everywhere is here,' said Jackal-Yackle Snickle-Snackle, 'I try to be in two places at the same time, but I can't do it like Stegalegs.'

'I don't get it.'

'Just because it is hard to understand doesn't mean it isn't true.'

Jackal-Yackle Snickle-Snackle hesitated. He pointed to a place where the river narrowed, and the cliffs on both sides leaned into each other so it was wider at the base than at the top. 'We're almost at the cliffs beside Silk Falls. The sky darkens. Soon we must stop to eat, to rest, to sleep before the final ascent.'

'You haven't told me how you stopped Chuzzle. Tell me what I want to know.'

Jackal-Yackle Snickle-Snackle pretended not to hear Jilly. He rushed ahead to where long strands of ivy dangled down the cliffs. He pulled back the greenery to reveal a dark space inside the rock.

Laughing, Zoa and Felicity-Blue dived in, 'This is Cockroach Cave. After the First Beanstalk crashed, we hid here from Chuzzle. We were silent for two full days, hardly daring to breathe. When Chuzzle passed nearby we heard him sniffing the air, but the cave smells terrible, of bats and cockroaches. It masked our scent.'

'When we fell, I hurt my butt,' interrupted Minto, the broad-shouldered boy with the scarred face. He rubbed his backside, remembering his bruises, then loped off to find suitable stones to put around the fire. Shtomp, in his round-rimmed sunglasses, fetched wood. Archer scooped dry leaves and dead grasses for kindling.

Joiner opened his knapsack and took out onions, garlic and baby potatoes, all covered in soil. He peeled off the skins with his rough hands, then crushed them between two flat stones. 'Mashed bits cook quick,' he explained to Jilly in a gruff voice.

'Can I help?' Jilly asked.

'There's a time to rest and a time to work,' said Jackal-Yackle Snickle-Snackle. 'Watch us do our work. You sit on that rock. Gather your strength for tomorrow.'

'What's happening tomorrow?'

Jackal-Yackle Snickle-Snackle said, 'The Amazing, I hope. Tomorrow maybe - or the day after. We have waited so long, we can be patient a few more hours.'

'You're making me nervous,' Jilly said.

The fire roared bright embers into the evening air. Lumber pulled a frying pan from his knapsack. In it, he tossed mushrooms, hazelnuts and parsley picked from the wayside. Joiner scraped the crushed potatoes, garlic and onions off the flat stone into the pan. Lumber held the pan over the fire and began to cook. The food released an enticing, delicious smell that drifted over Whey Wood. While they waited, the others found their tin mugs and went down to the riverside to fill them with water.

'Here,' Zoa said, offering her mug to Jilly, 'Drink.'

'Use my fork,' said Lumber, 'I'll eat with my fingers.'

The group huddled near the fire. Jilly noticed how the Fire-brothers were not afraid of the flames, despite their terrible experience as infants. When Lumber finished cooking, Minto took the pan and passed it round from friend to friend. Each one scooped a mouthful. Again, the pan went around, and many times more until everyone had had their fill.

'So few potatoes fed us all so well,' Jilly marvelled.

'That's because we share and no one is greedy,' said Zoa.

'Not too little, not too much, our food is always just enough,' chanted Shtomp, licking his lips. He removed his glasses and wiped the smoke off them. Jilly noticed that his eyes were scarred, and his eyebrows were long in some places and short in others, with bits missing.

Later, The Nine extinguished the fire then washed their hands and faces in Spinning River.

'I need to tell you all something,' said Jilly.

'Speak,' said Jackal-Yackle Snickle-Snackle.

'You go on about the Seed of the Stormflower, but I still don't know what that is. You seem to think I've got some kind of special power. I don't want to upset you, but I really don't have power. I'm just an ordinary girl. I can't save you. The only thing I brought with me was a net, but that was stolen by an invisible, talking cat, and . . .'

'Cats don't talk,' said Lumber.

'That'll be Chuzzle,' said Archer, yawning, showing the black space where he'd lost a tooth.

'She's seen Chuzzle,' agreed Joiner, signing with his hands as he spoke.

'Chuzzle's that cat you saw,' said Lumber.

'Well, you've got that all wrong,' said Jilly, 'Chuzzle is a wrinkly man with green hair and blue eyes. The cat's called Barker. He's a tabby with green eyes. He looks nothing like Chuzzle.'

'Chuzzle is whoever he wants to be,' said Zoa, 'He's very sneaky. He'd love to get to Skiddleyphet before us, but he can't because of you.'

'Why, what have I done?'

'You carry the Seed of the Stormflower which Chuzzle needs,' said Mr Jurado.

'And I keep telling you I don't.'

Zoa raised her hand. She had something serious to say, 'Ever since the fall of the First Beanstalk, Chuzzle has been searching for the seed that can never be destroyed. It is believed that the Seed of the Stormflower smells the same as Skiddleyphet. Nothing else on earth smells quite like it. Ordinary people like us cannot smell the seed, but Chuzzle's nose is more powerful than any dog. He can smell it. He knows you carry the seed, but if he stole it from you, the seed would instantly die. That's why, for now, he lets you keep it.'

'For now?'

'Yes, but soon you will plant it,' said Archer, pretending to fire an arrow into the sky. He followed the line of trajectory with his index finger, arching up, then down towards the ground.

'At the right time,' said Joiner, waving his hands to emphasise his words.

Felicity-Blue asked, 'I suspect Chuzzle gave you a gift. Something that smells of his sweat. Did he give you anything?'

'Not exactly,' said Jilly, shaking her head, 'Nope, he didn't give anything to me.'

'You don't seem too sure. Either he did or he didn't,' snorted Felicity-Blue, then turning to Zoa she added, 'I don't know why you trust this girl. She turns up out of nowhere, speaks the name of the eight-legged-one without respect, wears Jackal's shoes, refuses to dance, eats our food, knows nothing about the Stormflower, lies about Chuzzle . . .'

'I didn't lie,' stamped Jilly.

'You said he didn't give you anything, but I know he did.' Felicity-Blue peered deep into Jilly's eyes. Anger and mistrust shot between the two girls like electricity.

'He didn't.'

'Then why is there a cow in the distance?'

'Oh no, it's heading this way!' Jackal-Yackle Snickle-Snackle's face turned white, 'Quick, hide in the cave!' Everyone but Jilly shot into Cockroach Cave. They cowered in the shadowy darkness behind the overhanging greenery.

Jilly stood her ground. Felicity-Blue was being stupid about the cow. Cows are harmless. This one was no threat. It was a long way away down Piper's Path, and it was hardly moving,

innocently munching grass along the riverside.

'That'll be Nasuto. Black, white, eats grass, won't budge,' thought Jilly, 'I promised Chuzzle I'd whistle - I wonder if I can still do it.'

Jilly stuck her fingers in her mouth, pursed her lips and blew.

Deep in her pocket, the Seed of the Stormflower trembled.

7
Cockroach Cave

Chuzzle cartwheeled out of the brambles. He landed with both feet in the dying fire. 'Ooh, ouch, ouch!' he squealed. He jumped out, kicking hot ash all over the place. He shook the ash off his shoes. He clapped his hands, 'Griddling greatnesses, what a fabulous whistle! I wonder who taught you to whistle like that?'

'I've found your cow. She's over there.' Jilly pointed in the direction of Piper's Path, but Nasuto was nowhere to be seen. Jilly frowned, 'She was there, I promise.'

'Didn't anyone ever warn you not to make promises to me?' Chuzzle smiled. He cocked his head to one side then the other, like a cheeky robin, 'They didn't? Good. Now, young lady, I wonder where you're heading?'

'I'm not exactly sure.'

'Are you alone?'

'I wasn't. I am.'

'But I think you are not,' said Chuzzle raising his eyebrows. He blew on the ash and the ash glowed red. 'Eat by yourself? I don't think so.' He sniffed the air, 'It's a terrible thing to be all alone in the big, wide world.'

Jilly thought, 'He looks friendly enough. And he's only a wrinkly old man. He can't hurt me.' Then she remembered the rope. 'By the way, I found this when we met before,' she said, pointing to the rope around her waist, 'I tried give it to you, but you rushed off.'

'Keep it for now,' smiled Chuzzle, 'In fact, you may keep it for ever.'

'But you need it for Nasuto.'

'I said keep it,' insisted Chuzzle, 'It's my gift.'

Jilly dug her fingers into the tight knot, 'I can't undo it . . .'

'Keep it!' Chuzzle demanded.

Jilly pretended not to notice how angry he seemed. 'Okay, I'll ask Stegalegs to help me, he's good with ropes . . .' she said. She closed her eyes and whispered inside her head, *Stegalegs! I think I'm a tiny bit scared of Chuzzle. Where are you, Stegalegs?* Jilly looked up, 'I'm sure he won't be long . . .'

But Chuzzle had vanished.

Jilly scanned her eyes far down Piper's Path. And there it was again, the black and white cow munching on the damp grass beside the wide river.

Jackal-Yackle Snickle-Snackle stage-whispered from Cockroach Cave, 'Jilly!'

The Nine had remained so still and quiet that Jilly had forgotten all about them. She yelled at Jackal-Yackle Snickle-Snackle, 'You left me all by myself with Chuzzle!'

'Ssh, the others are sleeping,' said the boy, 'and you should rest too.'

'But Chuzzle . . .'

'Shush. He can't harm you while you have the Seed of the Stormflower.'

'But I don't have it.'

The boy cleared his throat. He shook his head as if to say, 'I know something you don't know,' then he said kindly, 'The way you sent Chuzzle packing was pretty impressive.'

'But I didn't.'

'You threatened him with You-Know-Who.' The boy wriggled his fingers like a spider walking.

'Stegalegs? Why would Chuzzle be afraid of Stegalegs? Chuzzle's a prince. Princes aren't supposed to be scared of anyone.'

'Did Chuzzle tell you that?'

'He says he's the Green Prince of Whey Wood.'

Jackal-Yackle Snickle-Snackle shook his head and laughed nervously, 'No more talk. Tomorrow we cross Silk Falls. It will be dangerous, but with your help we will make it.'

'Silk Falls? The falls at edge of the world? I've been there before. The water is deep and fast. You mustn't go over.'

'Don't worry, we'll be fine,' said Jackal-Yackle Snickle-Snackle, although he didn't seem too sure.

Jilly lay down on a mossy ledge close to Zoa. Exhaustion overwhelmed her and she fell into a restless sleep.

*

Early next morning, Jilly was the first to wake. Cockroach Cave smelt of musty mould and bat guano. The Nine were still asleep. Jackal-Yackle Snickle-Snackle lay curled like a kitten on the ground near the entrance of the cave. Sunlight poured in. It cast patterns of shadows and orange light over The Nine; triangles, squares and rectangles. A silverfish scuttled into a crack in the cave wall. Several cockroaches scurried beneath a rock. Jilly shivered. She stood up and stretched.

Streamers of ivy curtained the cave entrance, and something else - a silk net. 'So that's what's making those patterns,' smiled Jilly. She pressed her hand against the net, pushing it gently away. She dropped her hand and the net sprang back.

'This is the work of Stegalegs,' Jilly whispered, 'He protected us all night.' Through the web Jilly saw the rising sun shimmering on Spinning River. She pulled the web aside and stepped out into the morning light. She glanced up Piper's Path to check for Nasuto.

Nothing.

'I am not afraid,' she told herself as she wandered to the riverbank. She squatted close to the water's edge. She scooped freezing water in her cupped her hands to wash her face. A turquoise kingfisher flashed by. Dragonflies balanced on reed heads, flexing their wings to warm them. 'Oh!' Jilly cried, as an otter emerged on the far side of the river with a salmon flapping in its jaws. It loped into its holt beneath the overhanging bank. Jilly sensed a movement beside her. Her heart missed a beat. She swung around and looked up.

'Stegalegs!' spluttered Jilly, wiping her face on her sleeve.

'Don't hug me,' he warned, 'I'm not the hugging sort.'

'You're here!' Jilly jumped up, 'I knew you were close. I knew it!'

'I am always with you.'

Jilly talked quickly, 'The Nine think I can help them, but I haven't the foggiest idea what they're talking about.'

'You carry the Seed of the Stormflower.'

'You know about that stuff?'

'I do know.'

'Is it real – the seed, I mean?'

'Place your hand on your heart.'

Jilly obeyed. Something twitched in her breast pocket.

'It senses your heartbeat.'

'It's moving!' Jilly's hand shot away in fright.

'It is growing. The power is in the seed. Your destination is the Stormflower.'

Trembling, Jilly pulled open her pocket and looked down, trying to peer inside.

'Don't do that. Let it hide awhile longer in the dark.'

'How long for? When do I get to plant it? When?'

'First you must cross Silk Falls.'

'That's what Jackal-Yackle Snickle-Snackle said.'

'He will show you what to do.'

'But Spinning River . . .'

'It is dangerous, yes.'

'How will we cross without a bridge?'

'Trust me.' Stegalegs moved towards a clump of bulrushes, one leg after the other. 'Mmm, breakfast,' he whispered, 'my favourite meal of the day.'

'Flies?' asked Jilly. She could hear Stegalegs chomping as the bulrushes closed around him. Stegalegs shuffled through the bulrushes. As they rustled, their seeds blew like dandelion clocks into the wind.

*

'He's real!' Zoa clapped her hands with joy. Beside her, Felicity-Blue and the others had gathered outside Cockroach Cave. The

50

Nine had been standing shoulder to shoulder, watching Jilly in silent awe.

Mr Jurado stroked his long beard, 'Some of us doubted, some of us were certain, but none had ever set eyes on the beast before Jilly Jonah came.'

'He's not a beast, he's Stegalegs. Please say his name,' said Jilly, 'I say it all the time. He won't hurt you. Underneath those scary, hairy legs he's just one big softie.'

'Wow,' gasped Jackal-Yackle Snickle-Snackle, 'In all my life, I've never seen that kind of creature.' His tummy rumbled with hunger.

'Anyone for eggs?' asked Lumber, breaking half a dozen into the pan while the others lit a fire. They shared a giant omelette, passing the pan from one to the other as they did every day. Afterwards, in the same pan, Lumber boiled water. He poured it into mugs, adding nettle leaves, comfrey, or mint as they desired.

'I'm partial to parsley myself,' said Shtomp, picking a few tips from the hedgerow and stirring them with a twig.

Zoa softly sung the Song of Courage,
'Ohhhhhhh . . .
You don't know what you're doing here yet
You cannot catch a Fogling in a net
But you carry all we need
In a dark and tiny seed
To take us to the Land of Skiddleyphet.'

'I *didn't* know what I was doing, but do now,' insisted Jilly, 'I'm going to cross Silk Falls with you, climb the cliff, plant the Stormflower, grow the Stormflower, climb the Stormflower, find Skiddleyphet, go through the gates, then party!'

Felicity-Blue puffed out her cheeks and sneered, 'Aren't you a little-miss-clever-clogs. You think you know everything, but you don't.'

Zoa nudged her, 'Don't be mean, she can't help it. Jilly knows enough for today. Remember the ancient saying?'

Shtomp grinned at Felicity-Blue, 'Don't worry about tomorrow because today's trouble is enough to cope with.'

'That's exactly right,' nodded Minto and high-fived his brother.

'So,' said Mr Jurado, 'we will cross Silk Falls.'

Jackal-Yackle Snickle-Snackle skipped around the corner of the cliff. Jilly rose to follow.

Zoa held Jilly's arm, 'Don't rush after him. He'll won't leave us behind. He's only on a reccy.'

'Reccy?' Jilly screwed up her forehead.

'You know, checking things out. He likes to go before us,' laughed Zoa.

'That's our Jackal-Yackle Snickle-Snackle for you,' nodded Mr Jurado, combing his old-man's fingers through his drifting white beard.

'Ready for the off?' asked Archer, stretching back his bow. He pulled the string and released it without placing an arrow.

'Chop, chop,' said Joiner, making chopping motions with his hands and setting foot down the track.

'After you,' blushed Lumber, hitching up his trouser legs to stop them dragging in the dirt.

'Felicity-Blue, please help Lumber,' sighed Mr Jurado. The blue-haired girl squatted beside Lumber. She rolled his trousers up to his knees but as soon as she let go, they fell again.

'Safety pin?' she asked. Zoa had six safety pins linked together in a string on her knapsack. Zoa unclipped them and handed them over. Felicity-Blue pinned Lumber's trousers around his knees and he thanked her.

'Feels great,' he grinned, 'not to be flip-flapping like two flat fish.'

Minto and Shtomp linked arms and set off. The others followed. They rounded the bend. Suddenly Jackal-Yackle Snickle-Snackle reappeared.

'Sky, clear blue. Wind, zero. No storm on the horizon.'

'Tut, tut,' said Mr Jurado, 'Not good, not good at all.'

'I'd say that's great,' smiled Jilly, 'because the last thing we need is a storm.'

'No storm, no Stormflower. No Stormflower, no Skiddleyphet,' said Mr Jurado, shaking his head.

'We can shoot arrows, build bridges, cross rivers and plant seeds, but we can't make it rain. And now you're telling me that without rain we're doomed. I'm telling you that we can't make one raindrop fall from a single cloud, let alone crack open a full-on storm. So that's that then. We're stuffed. I should have stuck with Fogling catching.'

'Hup hem,' coughed Mr Jurado to Jackal-Yackle Snickle-Snackle, who winked back.

Jilly watched them making faces at each other. 'Are you mocking me?' she asked, but they shook their heads.

'Don't worry about what you cannot control,' said Mr Jurado, 'Run ahead, Jilly, while I guard the rear.'

To their left the river flowed. To their right, the cliffs towered, jagged in places, softer in others, a shelter for eagles, rodents, insects and crows. The far side of the riverbank was smothered in weeds and brambles. Above the riverbank, sheer cliffs were shadowed and treacherous.

But over the rushing waterfalls where the white gulls wailed, high above the clifftops, invisible to the human eye, lay the promise and hope of Skiddleyphet.

8
Catching the Canoe

Wild water raged over Silk Falls. Balls of white foam flew up and floated through the air. The river surged between ten jagged rocks that stuck up in a sharp curve of crocodile teeth.

'Ferocious,' said Mr Jurado.

'It's because of all that rain,' added Jackal-Yackle Snickle-Snackle. The Nine huddled together to discuss ways of crossing to the other side.

'Stepping-stones?' suggested Zoa.

'You've gotta be joking!' Shtomp snorted, 'I'll fall in - or else we all will.'

'Yeah. That green slime is super slippery,' said Minto.

Felicity-Blue sat down, kicked off her shoes and dipped her feet into the river. 'We ought to send know-all Jilly. Let her try it first since she thinks she's so great.'

Jackal-Yackle Snickle-Snackle sat down beside Felicity-Blue. He too lowered his feet into the water and sighed, 'Soooo good.'

Felicity-Blue snorted, 'Huh, look at your feet, all cut and bleeding. I bet you've got blisters too. I blame Jilly for taking your shoes.'

'But I wanted her to have them.'

'Stop defending her. She took them off you. She could have refused. She doesn't care about you one single bit.'

'She'd lost her trainers. If her feet hurt, she might have given up and gone home long ago.'

'Here,' said Jilly, who'd been eavesdropping from behind Jackal-Yackle Snickle-Snackle, 'Thanks a lot for these, but I'll be fine from now on.' She dropped the tatty, broken shoes between the boy and Felicity-Blue.

The boy protested, 'No!' but Jilly shook her head.

'I know what I'm supposed to do, and I know you think I'm soft. I don't need your dancing shoes anymore. Even if my feet are in agony I will never give up.'

Felicity-Blue glared at Jilly. 'Since you're so tough, we were thinking you should go first over Silk Falls.'

Jilly raised her eyebrows, 'I heard what you said, but that is never going to happen.'

'Hey, what's that?' yelled Lumber, pointing at a hollow log trapped in the water between some rocks, bashing between them as it bounced and whirled. It was far too big to go over the Falls.

'Wow!' cried Jilly and rushed to the water's edge, 'That's my canoe. I left it here last time I came.' The canoe spun in circles. A rope had been attached to a metal loop at the front of the canoe. It lashed out like a crazy eel. 'I'll grab it!' Jilly cried. She lay on her stomach to reach for the rope, stretching out until her nose was almost touching the water. When the canoe whirled close, her hand brushed against it but there was nothing to grip onto. The canoe rushed away. Jilly edged further over the bank, leaning, stretching . . .

'No!' yelled Zoa. Too late, Jilly slipped into the river. She kicked her legs like a frog and pulled back with her arms. The current spun her round and round, but Jilly held her head high, kept calm and powered on. She snatched the rope and caught it. Hand over hand, she hauled herself onto the nose of the canoe. She heaved over the nose then fell into the scooped-out middle, and sat hugging her knees to her chest, whirling and bumping from rock to rock.

Archer pulled back his bow and fired an arrow into the air.

'What are you doing, fool? You'll kill Jilly,' yelled Minto.

'What a pity he always misses,' shrugged Felicity-Blue. The arrow arced over Silk Falls and was gone. 'Told you he'd miss!' she smirked.

Archer shot a second arrow. This time it hit the canoe, rattling hard into its side. Still the canoe whirled. Archer lay flat on his stomach as Jilly had done before. He too reached out as the canoe passed near to him. He snatched at his arrow and held on tight. His knuckles turned white from gripping so hard. The arrow bent but remained stuck in the canoe.

Bang! The canoe stopped sharp. Jilly lurched forward. With both hands on the arrow, Archer hauled the canoe towards him. He clung to the arrow with all his might. Lumber managed to grab the rope and tie it to some tree roots. With the canoe secured, Shtomp and Minto grabbed Archer's ankles and pulled him to safety.

Zoa helped Jilly out of the canoe and onto the bank, 'How stupid was that? You almost drowned.'

'Not this time,' panted Jilly, 'but I had to get my canoe. Last time I was here, we had four canoes and . . .'

'We've no time for stories,' interrupted Jackal-Yackle Snickle-Snackle, 'Look!' He pointed to the horizon.

'What?' asked Jilly, glancing up.

'A cloud,' said Zoa.

'THE cloud,' said Mr Jurado in a booming voice that shocked Jilly.

'What cloud? I can only see sky,' said Jilly.

'That cloud there. The size of your fist,' said Zoa solemnly.

The Nine each raised a fist, palm out. They moved them horizontally before their eyes. 'The cloud is coming,' they chorused.

'Call that a cloud?' Jilly mocked. She squinted into the distance, 'It's no bigger than a ball of cotton wool. Storm clouds are huge and black and . . .'

Jackal-Yackle Snickle-Snackle picked up a stout stick. In the mud he drew an arch. 'First we build a bridge.'

Lumber's fist formed an arch in the air, 'The cloud appears. A bridge is built.'

Jilly snorted, 'With sticks?' but the others were already rushing here and there collecting branches, roots, rubbish - anything that had washed onto the riverbank or blown against the cliff.

'Don't just sit there, help us,' Zoa urged, tapping Jilly's

shoulder.

'No point,' said Jilly shaking her head, 'I'm no engineer, but one thing I do know, those sticks would make a better fire than a bridge. Even if you do make a bridge, it would be safer to cross in my canoe than on those skinny twigs.'

Mr Jurado beckoned Jilly over, 'Do not dishearten them. They're doing their best.'

'But they're rushing all over the place, wasting time and energy.'

'Well, what do *you* think they should do?'

'Think.'

'Then you must think for them,' said Mr Jurado, twirling his beard around his fingers, 'Go, Jilly Jonah, sit over there and think of what to do.'

*

Quietly in Jilly's pocket, the seed gave the green shoot the strength to grow.

9
Silk Bridge

The Nine collected rubbish; plastic bags, fishing tackle, hooks, bottles, a ripped coat, a soggy sock, a bent spoon, a broken gate. Altogether a disgusting pile of junk.

Jilly Jonah sat alone, staring at the terrifying gulf between the cliffs. The river swirled, the foam flew, and the Crocodile Teeth Rocks gnashed the river as if to say, 'See how vicious we are.'

'This is too hard for me,' thought Jilly, 'They only trust me because of a seed that I've never even seen!' Then she had another thought, 'What if the seed isn't real, after all? What if Stegalegs was joking and it isn't really in my pocket?' Jilly looked down at her pocket and pulled it open. Daylight flooded in. A curl of green leaves on a bright green stalk burst out and overflowed the pocket.

'How delicate it is,' whispered Stegalegs, though Jilly could not see him.

'Is the seed real?' asked Jilly.

'You cannot have a shoot without a seed.'

Jilly sighed, 'Mr Jurado told me to go away and think, but I don't know how.'

'If you could do *anything*, what would you do?'

An idea rushed into Jilly's mind and she blurted, 'I'd lie all those sticks and rubbish in a line. I'd get a super strong rope and wrap it around and around. Then I'd fly over Silk Falls and fix one end of the rope around the rocks or the trees, then I'd fly back and fix it over this side, then I'd do it again, then I'd drag the stuck-together sticks and rubbish . . .'

'Jilly!' cried Jackal-Yackle Snickle-Snackle, 'Come over here!' He was leaping all over the place, beckoning wildly.

Jilly looked up and saw an incredible sight. Her mouth fell open and her eyes widened, for there was a lumpy arch of dripping silvery thread spanning the Crocodile Teeth Rocks. The sun shone right through the translucent bridge, showing up all the junk inside - plastic bottles, empty toothpaste tubes, a shopping trolley, the garden gate, a bicycle wheel and a rotten window frame, sticks and grass, old clothes and so much more. Jilly rushed over to where Zoa was dancing with Felicity-Blue. Joiner high-fived Archer, and the Fire-brothers jigged a heavy-footed jig. Lumber and Mr Jurado stood side by side, shaking their heads in total amazement.

'Welcome to Silk Bridge,' announced Mr Jurado, 'and thank you, Jilly Jonah.'

'But I didn't do anything,' insisted Jilly, 'They did all the hard work collecting bits and pieces of junk.'

'True, I suppose you could say that their enthusiasm helped. Work is better than laziness and despair,' said Mr Jurado, 'but you made this more beautiful than work alone. You imagined our hope into reality.'

'How did she do that?' gasped Felicity-Blue.

'Some things can never be properly explained,' said Mr Jurado kindly.

Barefoot, Jilly stepped onto the bridge. The silk web stuck to the soles of her feet. Jilly lifted one foot then the other and the web pulled up like chewed gum. Everyone laughed.

Jilly stepped back onto dry land and chuckled, 'I give you the web of Stegalegs.' She began to pick sticky stuff off the soles of her feet.

Felicity-Blue approached Jilly with her head bowed, 'Here,' she said, 'I found these.'

'My trainers!'

'They were caught in the bulrushes. They must have travelled a long way from where you let them go.'

'Thank you, Felicity-Blue,' said Jilly, slinging them around her neck, 'When they're dry I'll put them on.'

'I'm sorry for not believing in you. Sorry for being a meanie.'

'I'm sorry too.'

'Friends?' asked Felicity-Blue.

'Fist bumps?' Jilly held up a fist. Felicity blushed. She pulled a face and jiggled her shoulders from one side to the other. Jilly said, 'Or no fist bumps?'

'Double fist bumps,' laughed Felicity-Blue, and the sun flashed sapphire in her hair.

*

Lumber patted Jilly on the shoulder. She turned to face him. Lumber blushed from his neck to his forehead. He nodded into the distance. *Look,* he said with his eyes, but he was choked with emotion and too shy to speak.

Jilly shrugged, 'What?'

'The clouds are gathering,' said Shtomp.

'We must cross without delay,' said Mr Jurado.

Jackal-Yackle Snickle-Snackle was already bouncing up and down on the springy bridge, not caring that the web stuck to him.

The friends gathered their belongings. They set off, eager to rush ahead, but politely allowing one another to go first. The stickiness meant no one would slide off into the river, but it was hard to lift one foot and then another.

Mr Jurado ran his fingers through his beard. He coughed gently, 'Walk with me, Jilly.' He took Jilly's arm and she did her best to lead him, but she felt impatient because he moved so slowly. Jilly watched as Zoa's head and shoulders vanished over the arch of the bridge ahead of them. Mr Jurado seemed to move even more slowly.

'My legs – so heavy – can hardly - walk,' he sighed. A gentle breeze blew over the bridge. Mr Jurado stopped. He gasped for air, clutching his hand to his chest.

'I can't carry you,' said Jilly, wishing she were stronger.

'You go on ahead, girl,' whispered Mr Jurado, 'I'll catch up - if I can.'

'No way,' said Jilly, though she longed to be with the others.

The breeze blew more strongly. The bridge wobbled.

'Then ask Stegalegs to help,' he wheezed.

'You said his name.'

'Did I?' Mr Jurado smiled. He fell to his knees, clutching his heart.

'Mr Jurado!' cried Jilly, but Mr Jurado reached up and pulled her until her ear was close to his mouth.

'Chuzzle will follow,' he rasped.

'What? I can't hear you,' said Jilly, as Mr Jurado fell face down upon Silk Bridge. His long silky beard blew in the breeze and flowed over both sides.

'Stegalegs help!' Jilly called, but her voice was drowned by the noise of the falling water. The bridge swayed and shook. Jilly knelt by Mr Jurado and held his hand. Jilly watched the raging water surge through the Crocodile Teeth Rocks, before spouting out to the bottomless space beyond.

The bridge wobbled violently. *Stomp, stomp, stomp.* Someone was coming.

Without warning, Mr Jurado was scooped into the air and cradled in Minto's chubby arms. Jilly too was lifted, 'Hey! Put me down!' she cried as Shtomp threw her over his shoulder in a fireman's lift. The bridge rattled and swayed beneath the heavy footsteps of the Fire-brothers.

Silk Bridge divided the clear blue sky over Whey Wood from the ominous dark clouds gathering on the far side of Silk Falls. The clouds swirled and swelled into shapes of galloping horses, snorting bulls, and roaring lions.

On the other side of Silk Bridge, Jackal-Yackle Snickle-Snackle waited, hands on hips. His next task would be to lead The Nine along a narrow path up the steep, towering cliff. Countless gulls nested in every nook and cranny of the cliff face. Others circled overhead, crying. Long-horned goats balanced on tiny hooves as they leapt from ledge to impossible ledge.

No one danced. No one sang. No one even spoke. They watched Shtomp and Minto carry Jilly and Mr Jurado towards them. At last, Shtomp put Jilly down. He took Mr Jurado from his brother and rocked him in his arms. The others gathered round.

'Has he . . . has he . . . died?' sobbed Zoa. She laid her head on Mr Jurado's chest. His beard tickled her ear. Zoa sighed with relief, 'He is breathing, but he is weak.' Zoa lifted her head, 'Come on, friends. We must keep going.'

Shtomp plodded on, with Mr Jurado's feathery beard cascading over his arms.

No one noticed Jilly lagging further and further behind. She tripped over a stick and grazed her hands on the stony path. She stood up and was about to kick the stick angrily when she realised that it wasn't a stick at all. It was a big, square-headed net.

'My Fogling-catcher!' she cried and tried to pick it up. For some strange reason it was weighed down. Something heavy seemed to be in the net. Hovering above was a swaying half-moon of white stones.

'You again! I know who you are, you sneaky thief. Just because I can't see you doesn't mean I don't know who you are. Get out of my net this minute!' yelled Jilly.

'Touchy, touchy. How about being polite. You might like to say thank-you very much Barker,' said Barker, 'for being so kind as to carry my net all this way just for me.'

'But you stole it.'

'Borrowed.'

'Stole.'

'Borrowed for your own good. You can't go carrying massive black nets up Spinning River. You'll scare the life out of the Foglings, the poor little things.'

'I can do what I like.'

'And I say you can't.'

'Whatever. Get out of my net.'

'I will, I will,' said the white stones. The net shook. 'I must say huge congratulations to you for constructing such a wonderful bridge. I wonder who helped you?'

Jilly tugged at the net. It was still heavy, 'Get – out – now!'

'I am, I will. Some things take time. I bet you've forgotten what this net was for?'

'I have not.'

'Tell me.'

'To catch a Fogling.'

'But you abandoned your dream. Why? You gave your own fun up because a bunch of strangers flattered you into helping them. And what did they give you in return? Zilch. Nada. Nuttin.'

'Nothing.'

'That's what I said.'

'You said nuttin.'

'Nuttin, nothing, it's all the same to me. Here's the deal,' said the white stones, 'I get out of your net and you can have it back if you promise to hide in the bulrushes until they've gone. Then go back over the bridge. Go, catch yourself a bitty, little Fogling. I promise you, if you hurry, you will catch one first thing in the morning.'

Jilly tugged at the net. It was so unexpectedly light that she fell backwards. Barker had disappeared. Jilly picked herself up. She swiped the air with the net. It felt good to have control again. Turning her back on the Nine, she cried, 'Foglings here I come!'

*

Something twitched against her heart. Jilly looked down. The skinny green shoot was growing fast, twisting out of her breast-pocket, tumbling almost down to her waist. 'Oh,' she gasped, 'I totally forgot about the Stormflower!' Above the bridge, the sky darkened. Jilly shuddered. She looked at her net, then back at the bridge. The bridge rocked in the wind.

'If I don't go back immediately, the bridge will break and I'll be too late,' said Jilly to her net, 'I'm going to chuck the stupid seed into Spinning River. Barker was right. I shouldn't have to give up my own dream to help people I hardly know.' Jilly looked for The Nine, but they had walked ahead without her. 'They left me behind. Chuzzle was right, as soon as they crossed their precious bridge, they forgot me. They don't need me anymore, at least, I don't think they do.'

Jilly took a step back onto the bridge. It rocked. The middle was sinking. It had slumped so it was almost touching the roaring river.

'What shall I do? Stegalegs, what shall I do?' Jilly called into the wind. She felt very small and very alone.

*

The skinny shoot grew longer, and the wind whipped it around Jilly's legs.

10
A Tough Choice

Jilly felt a hand on her shoulder. She swung round to see Jackal-Yackle Snickle-Snackle. The boy slammed his hands onto his hips. He was tapping his foot and looked furious.

'Hey, Jilly Jonah, we've been waiting ages for you.'

'You didn't wait for me at all. You left me.'

'We thought you were with us. I've had to leave them on their own to come back and find you. What are you playing at?'

'The bridge is breaking. If I don't go back right now, I'll never catch a Fogling!'

'What about us? You have the Seed of the Stormflower. See how the shoot curls from your pocket reaching almost to the ground? The seed must soon be buried.'

'You can have your precious seed. I didn't ask for it in the first place.'

'You know I can't touch it. We need you, Jilly Jonah.'

'Well, I don't need you. And what about my Fogling? Barker promised me I'll definitely catch one in the morning.' Jilly leant heavily upon the net-head and the handle sunk into the bridge.

Jackal-Yackle Snickle-Snackle backed slowly away. He was no longer bouncing. His shoulders slumped. His hand covered his mouth because he had no words. He blinked back tears, 'You listened to Chuzzle.'

Jilly sighed, 'I wish Stegalegs was here. He'd tell me what to do.'

'You don't need him or anyone else to tell you what to do. You already know what is right,' said Jackal-Yackle Snickle-Snackle.

'I came to catch a Fogling,' whispered Jilly.

Jackal-Yackle Snickle-Snackle turned sadly away. He

dragged his feet. The frayed string on his shoes trailed in the dirt. 'The clouds are gathering,' he called. Fat raindrops landed on the bridge with a loud 'plap, plap, plap.'

Jilly wiped a raindrop from her cheek. She faced her net, 'Forget about that boy. I've made up my mind. From now on, it's you and me against the world. We're going to catch a Fogling!' Jilly yanked the net, but it had sunk deep into the sticky bridge. With both hands she pulled with all her might, and roared, 'My net! My dream! My Fogling!' but the net was stuck fast. Jilly let go. The net pinged wildly back and forth. Breathing heavily, Jilly tried again to remove it.

All the while the small boy wandered further away. The elastic band from his ponytail had fallen off so his hair blew in the breeze. The fringes of his jacket and his baggy trousers flapped like a torn sail on a stricken yacht.

Jilly tugged and pulled at the net until she was exhausted. She looked up just in time to see Jackal-Yackle Snickle-Snackle disappearing into the undergrowth at the foot of the cliff.

She thought sadly, 'He was kind to lend me his terrible shoes. I told him I'd never give up, but I did.'

The shoot of the Stormflower whipped against Jilly's face. It made her look up. Along the borders of the path where Jackal-Yackle Snickle-Snackle had just been, Nasuto was munching quietly, flicking her tail against flies. 'How odd,' Jilly thought, 'Nasuto is on that side of the river. I've been here all the time and I never saw her cross Silk Bridge.'

With one hand on the net, and the other wrapped around the rope about her waist Jilly told herself, 'I promised Chuzzle I'd whistle if I saw Nasuto. I ought to whistle. It's only fair.' She put her fingers to her mouth, but she hesitated.

'Something's wrong,' she said, 'Jackal-Yackle Snickle-Snackle asked me if Chuzzle gave me a gift. He believes Chuzzle is trying to trick me.' Jilly looked down at the rope, 'But this is all Chuzzle gave me. It's not a gift. It's a piece of junk. It's only what Chuzzle used to lead his cow with. But he did refuse to take it when I tried to give it back. If Chuzzle can smell his scent on this rope, he'd turn up here whether I whistle or not.' Jilly looked around nervously for the strange man, but he was nowhere to be seen.

Jilly relaxed. 'I'm worrying about nothing. First, I'll catch a Fogling then, if Silk Bridge is still here tomorrow, I might come back to find The Nine to find out how they're getting on, or I might not.'

The instant Jilly decided to abandon The Nine, the net broke free. 'Yay!' cried Jilly. She waved it triumphantly over her head and set off back over Silk Bridge.

*

Thunder grumbled overhead. Silk Bridge slumped. Its underside touched the surface of the river. The water rushed by, fierce and fast. Jilly's heart pumped with fear. She could even feel it throbbing in her neck! Using the net for balance she struggled to stay upright and not fall in, even with sticky feet.

High above and far away, someone called her name, 'Jilly!'

'Stegalegs?' Jilly asked, although she knew it was not him.

'Jilly!' The call was louder than before. Not one voice, but many voices. Jilly peered in the direction of the sound. There, far away on a ledge, halfway up the cliff face, were The Nine, like tiny dolls waving for all they were worth. Jilly could just about make out Felicity-Blue's hair, and Mr Jurado's beard, and the broad shoulders of Minto and Shtomp.

'Jilly, Jilly, Jilly!' they cried as loud as they could above the thunder.

Jilly waved weakly, wondering if they could see her. 'This is my dream,' she stammered, knowing they could not hear. She hugged the net to her body. 'I want to catch a Fogling, but you want me to plant a seed. I don't do gardening.' Jilly looked at her net, then at the raging water spurting through the Crocodile Teeth Rocks.

High on the cliff side Jackal-Yackle Snickle-Snackle was bouncing again, waving his hands and screaming 'Jilly, Jilly!' Jilly could hear the others laughing at him, egging him to scream louder.

'One, two, three, J – i – l – l - y!' cried The Nine. *Now* what were they doing? Singing the Song of Courage. It began softly, then grew louder and louder.

'Ohhhhhh!
You don't know what you're doing here yet
You cannot catch a Fogling in a net
But you carry all we need
In a dark and tiny seed
To take us to the Land of Skiddleyphet.'

The song rode the wind. It bounced between the cliffs and echoed through the mountains, and melted Jilly's heart.

'I miss them,' whispered Jilly, 'and they need me. I broke my promise to Jackal-Yackle Snickle-Snackle. I said, "Even if my feet are in agony I'll never give up," but I broke my promise.' Jilly raised the net back over her shoulder like a javelin and roared as, with all her might, she threw it over Silk Falls. The net flapped out behind like a bat on a broomstick.

Jilly watched the net rise. At its height it hung. Then down, down, down it fell, into the abyss until it was out of sight.

*

Tiny leaves formed along the skinny shoot of the Stormflower as it dragged over the rough earth.

11
Don't Look Down

'I'm free!' cried Jilly. She leapt off Silk Bridge just as it slumped further into the river. Water hit the middle of the bridge. It gushed up and over it. The weight of water stretched the sticky silk at each side of the bridge. Jilly ran to where Nasuto was grazing. She sped past the cow without looking back. She found an animal track winding between rocks and scrubby bushes. It led Jilly onto the narrow path that led up the cliff face.

'Wait for me!' she cried, trying to run, but gasping for breath. The path became so narrow that Jilly was forced to stop. 'I'm scared,' she said, 'And my feet hurt.'

'Trainers?' A quiet word in her mind.

'Yes, yes,' Jilly said. Her fingers trembled as she untied the knot. She was amazed to find her socks in the larger pocket across her stomach. She pulled on her warm socks and then the damp trainers. 'I can do this,' she said as she struggled to her feet, 'I can do it.'

Jilly pressed her back against the cliff and edged sideways, step by slow step, higher and higher. 'Don't look down, don't look down,' she repeated so many times that her mouth went dry. The eagle swept by so close Jilly felt the wind beneath its wide wings. Jilly trudged on, each step more terrifying than the last, 'Don't look down, don't look down.' Above her, the golden bird settled on its eerie, knocking feathers and twigs over the ledge. A small stone tumbled and bounced over Jilly, narrowly missing her head. She kept moving, inch by terrifying inch.

'Zoa?' Jilly called, but Zoa could not hear her above the howling wind. Jilly came to a wider part of the path. She rested for a moment and dared to look down. Far below, Spinning River snaked back past the cliffs and waterfalls to Hamelin Lake. And beyond the lake lay Whey Wood, with its tall trees and rambling brambles. Further on, Whey House glowed orange beneath an enormous tangerine sun.

Jilly felt dizzy. She placed her palms back against the damp cliff, feeling for small rocks to grip. The path became steep steps, some higher than Jilly's head. She hauled herself up using both hands, scraping her knees on jutting rock. She remembered not to squash the delicate green shoot that tumbled from her pocket. She flicked it back over her shoulder. The ragged roots of a tenacious tree poked through the rocks. Jilly clambered up the roots and found a split in the rock face. The crack was shaped like a diagonal chimney. Jilly squeezed in and pressed her palms and her thighs against each side. She forced herself up, little by little. Sweat poured down her forehead into her eyes. She gritted her teeth and kept climbing.

Voices. Chattering. Wedged within the rock, Jilly looked up at the darkening sky. 'Hello?' she called.

'She's down there!' someone called.

'Here,' said Archer, leaning over and peering down. He and Joiner reached down and scooped Jilly up. Jilly stumbled out of the chimney and collapsed on the clifftop. She lay back, panting with relief, as The Nine stared down at her.

'See how the shoot of the Stormflower grows,' said Zoa.

'Yet it looks weak somehow,' said Felicity-Blue.

'It awaits the rain,' said Archer.

'It longs for the strength and faithfulness of the new beanstalks,' said Jackal-Yackle Snickle-Snackle.

'And I need to lie down,' said Mr Jurado.

12
Strong and Faithful

Mr Jurado rested among the pile of worn rucksacks, pots and pans, and bow and arrows. A mound of rough stones sheltered him from the worst of the wind.

'Those stones are called a cairn,' explained Zoa to Jilly.

'Cairns are places which help us remember the past,' added Felicity-Blue, 'This cairn was built by those who were about to climb the First Beanstalk. Each stone was carried here from Spinning River as a thank offering for a safe passage to Skiddleyphet.'

'The First Beanstalk,' said Jackal-Yackle Snickle-Snackle, 'was our stairway to Skiddleyphet. Thousands climbed, or were carried up to the Gleaming Gate. We were the last in line. It would have been perfect . . .'

'But for Chuzzle,' said Archer.

'Chuzzle turned up,' said Joiner, signing thumbs-down.

'He wants to rule Skiddleyphet,' added Lumber.

Jackal-Yackle Snickle-Snackle picked up a stone and tossed it onto the cairn. It landed with a loud click. 'We had planned to visit this spot every year, but we never came back. Thinking of these stones gave us hope.'

'What is hope?' Jilly asked.

'Hope is things not yet seen.'

'Like Skiddleyphet?'

'Yes. And The Amazing. I hope soon to see The Amazing.'

'Look!' cried Lumber, shielding his eyes with his hand. On the distant horizon, an electrical spark hit the earth.

The Nine counted very loudly, 'One, two, three, four, five, six, seven, eight, nine, ten.' Thunder gurgled over the land.

'Ten miles,' murmured Mr Jurado, 'The storm is coming.'

Jackal-Yackle Snickle-Snackle knelt at the foot of the cairn. He brushed away twigs of dry heather. 'Here,' he said, creating a circle of rich red earth with his hands, 'This is the place of planting.' From his pocket he withdrew four kidney-shaped beans.

'Select only the best two,' wheezed Mr Jurado.

Jackal-Yackle Snickle-Snackle rubbed four beans between his palms. He lifted each one close to his face to inspect it. He smelt them. Placed the tip of his tongue against them. 'I had five beans, but I tasted one. Bleagh! Spat it out. It needed boiling.'

'Did you sell Nasuto for those beans?' Jilly asked, remembering the bean-spit all over her hoodie.

'What do you think?' asked Jackal-Yackle Snickle-Snackle, 'You asked me that before. I told you there are no cows in Whey Wood. You still don't trust me, do you? Chuzzle lied to you. He lies all the time. He lives a lie. He IS a lie.'

'So, if Chuzzle didn't give you the beans, where did you get them?'

'When we cut down the First Beanstalk I snapped a bean-pod from it. Inside the pod were five beans. I've kept them safe for all these years. We would never take a thing from Chuzzle, not a single bean. Not in a million years. Nothing Chuzzle says or does is good or true.'

'But why do you need *two* beans?'

'Two beans plus the Stormflower,' wheezed Mr Jurado, 'One alone is weak, two are better, but a three-fold cord can withstand all attack. As the ancient saying goes, "A cord with three strands cannot be broken." The First Beanstalk did a brilliant job but, when Chuzzle attacked, it had to be destroyed.'

'So why don't you use three beans? Why do you need the Stormflower?'

'Okay, so one bean is strong. The other is faithful. The strong one gives strength in tough times. The faithful stay together forever,' said Zoa, 'And the Stormflower . . .'

'The Stormflower is selfless,' said Mr Jurado, 'This is the opposite of Chuzzle. He only thinks about himself.'

Zoa nodded, 'Your selflessness fed the seed.'

'But I wanted to do what I wanted when I wanted. How's that selfless?'

'You desperately wanted to catch a Fogling, but you gave up your dream to help us.'

'Look again, there!' cried Jackal-Yackle Snickle-Snackle. Another lightning flash. The Nine counted, 'One, two, three, four, five, six, seven, eight, nine,' and the thunder grumbled.

'Nine miles. The storm is coming,' wheezed Mr Jurado. Felicity-Blue offered him water from her tin mug. He lifted his head for a sip then lay back to rest.

Jackal-Yackle Snickle-Snackle smoothed the red earth with the palm of his hand. He planted the two most perfect beans in the centre. He patted the earth over them. No one spoke. They bowed their heads and waited.

Flash!

'One, two, three, four, five, six, seven, eight,' they chanted. The thunder cracked.

'Eight miles,' said Mr Jurado.

Zoa clapped her hands, 'Hurry Jilly, it's your turn now.' Jilly looked puzzled. Felicity-Blue said, 'Plant the Seed of the Stormflower.'

'Gently plant our Storm-flower,' said Shtomp, concerned about the delicate shoot that overflowed Jilly's pocket and curled down to her ankles.

Jilly pulled her pocket open. Her heart thumped against her ribs. She felt in her pocket for the precious seed. Held it up between her thumb and forefinger. Inspected it. She could not hide her disappointment. The seed was small and brown and split in two. The shoot had grown too fast. It hung weakly over her hand. Jilly stuck out her bottom lip, 'After all that, it's half dead.'

'That is one good seed,' gasped Minto.

'I was expecting it to be beautiful,' said Jilly.

'It is perfect,' smiled Zoa.

Everyone held their breath as Jilly laid the seed on the ground. Its bruised shoot flopped out over the ground like a pale green grass-snake.

'I may have squashed it against the rock,' she confessed. Jilly covered the seed with a handful of earth.

'It needs a drink,' said Zoa, 'but there is no water up here.'

'Lightning!' cried Felicity-Blue, turning to the horizon to see.

'One, two, three, four, five, six, seven.'

Jackal-Yackle Snickle-Snackle opened his hands to the heavens. Two large raindrops fell, one in the centre of each hand. Drop by drop the rain fell on the clifftop. All eyes were upon the circle of earth. Rain spotted the circle. One bean pushed a tiny shoot up through the soil. The second quickly followed. Each grew a leaf. Still, the shoot of the Stormflower lay motionless, thin and weak.

'Is it dead? Are we too late?' asked Zoa, with tears in her eyes.

'Or too early?' asked Felicity-Blue.

'Lightning!' cried Minto and Shtomp, filling their arms around one another's shoulders.

'One, two, three, four, five, six.'

Thunder.

A second leaf appeared from each bean, then a third. Soon the beans were growing fast, intertwining, until they stood higher than the cairn, higher than Jilly, taller even than Archer. Curly tendrils reached from one stalk to the other, tying knots, supporting one another. Still the Stormflower stretched flat and exhausted over the earth.

'We're too late,' said Zoa.

'Lightning!' cried Joiner, zig-zagging his hand to the earth.

'One, two, three, four, five.' The thunder roared.

Jilly saw that the sun was sinking behind the distant chimneys of Whey House. Orange and gold light speared across a navy sky.

'Lift the shoot, Jilly,' said Jackal-Yackle Snickle-Snackle.

'Me?'

'Only you can touch it. That's why Chuzzle didn't steal it from you. Only the one who is genuinely selfless may do this.'

With shaky hands Jilly lifted the shoot, cradling it carefully, trying not to pull it or snap it. She pressed it gently against the growing beanstalks. The top of the shoot flopped over her hand.

'Hold on, Jilly,' urged Zoa.

'But it's not moving,' said Jilly, 'I can't feel it twitching like it did before.' She blinked back tears, 'It's dead and it's all my fault. I tried to leave you. I wasted time trying to pull the net out of Silk Bridge. I wanted what I wanted. I stopped caring about you.'

'Breathe on it,' croaked Mr Jurado though his eyes were shut. Felicity-Blue knelt beside the old man. She held his hand to comfort him.

Jilly breathed on the shoot and whispered, 'I was selfish. I'm so sorry.'

Lightning flashed.

'One, two, three, four,' cried The Nine, and the thunder clapped. 'Oh, that is sooo close.'

Jilly squealed, 'The Stormflower twitched!'

Everyone stared but they only saw how limp and floppy it hung.

'I can't see it moving,' said Shtomp.

'Me neither,' shrugged Minto.

'Hush,' said Jackal-Yackle Snickle-Snackle.

'There, I felt it again,' grinned Jilly. Heavy raindrops fell on the seed, the seed absorbed the water, and the water rose through the shoot. The shoot swelled. It straightened. It did not curl like the beanstalks but grew upright, straight and tall. The beanstalks wrapped their long tendrils around the Stormflower shoot from bottom to top.

Jilly Jonah pressed her cheek to the shoot and whispered, 'Grow, Stormflower, grow.' The shoot sent out a leaf, covered in tiny hairs. A seven-spot red ladybird landed on the leaf.

Lightning.

Jilly let go of the Stormflower. She stepped back.

'One, two, three,' cried The Nine. Thunder clattered. All but Mr Jurado gathered their rucksacks and tin mugs and pans and clipped them to their knapsacks.

Mr Jurado lay quietly with his eyes closed. He beckoned Jilly over, 'I've waited, oh so long, for this moment.' A single tear of happiness ran down his cheek.

13
Fire and Water

The clouds looked grey against the navy sky. The Stormflower shot up into the clouds and beyond until the Nine could no longer see the bud.

'I can see red flowers that look like butterflies!' cried Jilly, because hundreds of scarlet petals had opened all the way up the beanstalks. The Stormflower bore no flowers, but only huge hairy leaves attached to the stalk by their own sturdy leafstalks.

'Bean-flowers,' said Zoa, 'aren't they stunning?'

Lightning.

'One, two,' everyone cried. Thunder roared.

'The storm is only two miles away. We must climb without delay. Light the storm-lanterns,' commanded Jackal-Yackle Snickle-Snackle.

Shtomp and Minto produced six solar-powered photovoltaic copper-based storm-lanterns[1], and attached each one to a hook on a short pole. Minto flicked the switches. Sunlight that had been absorbed by the solar panels for many years was released. The beanstalks and the Stormflower cast huge leafy shadows onto the clouds. And in the warm light of the storm-lanterns, the faces

---

1 Solar-powered photovoltaic (PV) panels convert the sun's rays into electricity by exciting **electrons** in silicon cells using **photons** of light from the sun. Sounds complicated? Don't worry, one day you'll get it!

of The Nine glowed amber.

'Won't Chuzzle see the light and find us?' asked Zoa, suddenly worried and looking about.

'I doubt it. His sight is poor. He prefers to use his nose. He needs scent to follow us – his own scent. We don't have anything that smells of Chuzzle so don't stress,' grinned Jackal-Yackle Snickle-Snackle.

'Except . . . I . . . I think I do,' mumbled Jilly, thinking how stupid it was to worry about a piece of old rope. She didn't know why she kept it - she just did. No one heard her, so Jilly quickly changed the subject. She pointed to the old man asleep at her feet and said loudly, 'What's going to happen to Mr Jurado? He'll never be able to climb the Stormflower. He can hardly stand up.'

'True. But who helps us when we cannot help ourselves?' winked Jackal-Yackle Snickle-Snackle mysteriously, 'Lead on, Felicity-Blue.'

Shtomp fastened one of the storm-lanterns onto a pole. He slid the pole into a special pouch on Felicity-Blue's rucksack. The storm-lantern shone a halo over Felicity-Blue's head.

'You look beautiful, Felicity-Blue,' said Jilly.

'Thanks,' said the blue-haired girl. Felicity-Blue found a foothold between the beanstalks and the Stormflower and hauled herself up. Giving a thumbs-up she called, 'Thank you, Jilly Jonah. See you at the Gleaming Gate!'

Shtomp gave Felicity-Blue a head start, then he set off climbing. By now, all three stalks had grown so thick he could not wrap his arms all the way around. Minto went next, carrying a storm-lantern. 'See you at the Gleaming Gate, Mr Jurado,' called Minto, 'I hope.' He blinked back tears and saluted the sleeping gentleman.

Jackal-Yackle Snickle-Snackle turned to Jilly. He pulled his long hair back and twisted it into a knot to make a ponytail. His face was serious. 'You brought us the seed. You walked in my shoes. You gave up your dream for us. For that we are grateful.'

'It's not such a big deal,' shrugged Jilly.

'There is one more thing we need you to do.'

'And then will you show me the amazing thing?'

Jackal-Yackle Snickle-Snackle sounded impatient, 'Please stop calling it a thing. It's not a thing. It's An Amazing. I can't show you, not yet. Trust me, it will happen. But first we need your help.'

'Did you lie to me about the amazing thing - I mean, The Amazing - just to make me follow you?' asked Jilly.

Jackal-Yackle Snickle-Snackle blinked. He looked as if he was going to cry. 'Lie? Never! The Nine always tell the truth. If you don't believe me after all we've been through, you might as well go home.'

Archer felt the tension rising. He interrupted, 'Um, Jilly's right. Mr Jurado is too weak to climb. He will need a silver hammock this time.'

'Last time the hammocks just kind of happened,' shrugged Joiner, opening his hands to express his amazement.

Zoa said, 'We guessed it was You-Know-Who, but we're not a hundred percent sure.'

'You guessed it was Stegalegs? Of course, it was Stegalegs,' said Jilly.

'Which is why we need you to ask him to help Mr Jurado,' said Lumber, blushing.

Jilly frowned, 'Why me?'

'Because he's your friend and you're not scared of him,' said Jackal-Yackle Snickle-Snackle.

'He's your friend too.'

'I . . . I'm not sure. We haven't time to find out. Please Jilly, ask You-Know-Who for a hammock for Mr Jurado.'

Bang! On the far side of the river, lightning struck a huge oak tree. The branches of the tree exploded into a million pieces, shooting splinters in all directions.

'One mile to go!' cried The Nine, 'The storm is almost above us!'

From high on the Stormflower stalk Felicity-Blue yelled, 'Hurry up down there. We must all meet at the top of the Stormflower before the last lightning strikes.'

Thunder cracked and rumbled long and loud, like a pride of circling lions. On and on it grumbled. Jilly noticed that Jackal-Yackle Snickle-Snackle's face had turned as white as a sheet. His brown eyes begged her to do this one last thing, to ask Stegalegs to send a silver hammock for Mr Jurado.

Inside her head, despite the thunder and the fear, Jilly heard the voice of Stegalegs, 'They must ask, or they will never know me for themselves.'

'Do it!' begged Jackal-Yackle Snickle-Snackle.

'What are you waiting for?' Zoa looked angry, 'Don't you care about Mr Jurado?'

'I want to, but I can't,' said Jilly.

'Of course, you can,' Lumber brought his face close to Jilly's, 'It's easy for you. Do it to save Mr Jurado!'

Jilly trembled. They were right, it would be easy for her. All she had to do was ask, or even imagine, Stegalegs to send a hammock and, just like Silk Bridge, it would happen.

'You're being so stubborn!' yelled Archer. Even he was frustrated by her refusal.

'No,' said Jilly firmly, 'you must do it. One of you, or all of you. I cannot.'

Joiner tried a gentler approach. He laid his hands upon Jilly's shoulders and did his best to sound kind, 'Stop messing and just get on with it, Jilly.'

Jilly shook her head, 'Sorry, I can't.'

From high up the Stormflower, Minto and Shtomp shouted down, 'Fire! Fire!' The oak tree that had been hit by lightning was burning. Flames licked the night, sending sparks of ash towering into the sky. The huge raindrops that were falling were not enough to extinguish the fire.

'See what you've done, Jilly?' yelled Jackal-Yackle Snickle-Snackle, 'You made me really angry and now there's a fire.'

Jilly watched the tree burn. It was terrifying and beautiful at the same time. 'I didn't cause the fire. That was the lightning, not me, and you know it.'

'Mr Jurado collapsed on the bridge because he spoke the

name we must not mention. Because of you, we've been saying that name all over the place like it's no big deal. We warned you it was dangerous. Now Mr Jurado is weak and dying. We can't risk asking You-Know-Who.'

'Wrong again,' said Jilly, 'Mr Jurado fell down because he is old.'

'Jilly!' Zoa spat, 'That's quite enough talk. We're wasting precious time. If you don't hurry up and ask Stegalegs for the silver hammock, I'll do it myself!'

*

A massive cloud burst open. Rain poured down in buckets, drenching The Nine and drenching Jilly, and drenching the burning tree. The fire hissed like a thousand snakes. As the flames died, Zoa cried, 'Look at that!' She pointed to where Mr Jurado lay. A silver hammock with a silk rope on each corner had lowered from nowhere. It was rocking close to where Mr Jurado lay.

Jilly said, 'You did that, Zoa. You asked Stegalegs. He did this because of you.'

'But I never said a thing,' Zoa argued. Her mouth hung open in astonishment.

'You said his name. You accidentally asked Stegalegs for help,' said Jilly, 'and that was enough for him to hear and answer you.'

'Give me a hand,' Archer called to Joiner. The brothers lifted Mr Jurado into the hammock. In the hammock was a silver blanket. Lumber covered the old man with it, as Felicity-Blue held Mr Jurado's hand.

'Stand back,' said Archer.

'Goodbye my friend,' whispered Felicity-Blue, 'Be safe.' Everyone watched in awe as the hammock ascended alongside the beanstalks and the Stormflower.

'Let's go!' cried Jackal-Yackle Snickle-Snackle, feeling much relieved, 'I love climbing, I simply love it. I told you before, so you know how much I love it!' One after the other the friends climbed, some with storm-lanterns rocking above their heads to light the way for the one below. Jilly was the last to leave the clifftop. With both hands she grabbed hold of the stalk of the Stormflower. It felt stronger than any tree. Jilly found a foothold where the beanstalks twisted around it. She heaved herself up. She felt for the next foothold, then pressed her cheek against the shoot. It was covered in fine, damp hairs and smelt as fresh as newly cut grass. Jilly was certain she could feel it growing thicker and taller by the second.

The Stormflower shuddered under the weight of the climbers. They moved as quickly as they could because the last lightning was sure to strike at any time.

From just beneath her feet, Jilly heard a familiar voice, 'Hellooooo!'

Jilly froze.

'It's only me, Chuzzle, the famous Green Prince of Whey Wood.'

14
The Cheat and the Stormflower

Jilly felt Chuzzle's breath on her ankles.

'Let me pass, or I'll climb over you,' he grinned.

'Don't you dare,' Jilly said, kicking out at Chuzzle's face.

Chuzzle ducked and laughed. Gripping a beanstalk with one hand, Chuzzle hung out and looked up, 'I can't see the head of the Stormflower through those clouds. All I want is a mini, skinny glimpse of the future. It's not too much to ask for, is it? Go on, I beg you, let me pass.'

'You're not supposed to go there,' Jilly insisted. She also looked up. The underside of Mr Jurado's silver hammock rose higher and higher until it was a speck against the grey clouds.

Chuzzle coughed, 'Oy, stop looking up. Look down here. You're not paying me proper attention. I go where I choose and so should you.'

'You can't go ruining other people's lives just so you can be important.'

'Important? Huh! I'll be more than important. I'll be greater than any king. I, Chuzzle, Green Prince of Whey Wood will become president, mayor and ruler of all Skiddleyphet. Crowds will cheer as I enter the Gleaming Gate.'

Jilly took a deep breath. She pulled herself up, wedging her trainers in the gaps between the twisted shoots. She looked down. Chuzzle hadn't moved. 'Strange,' she said out loud. She climbed again. Now he followed her, appearing below her, hanging out from the beanstalk, constantly checking, peering upwards for a gap in the clouds.

Jilly moved up again. Chuzzle waited. Jilly moved again, and he followed. Not once did he touch so much as the sole of her trainer. 'It's as if he is afraid of me,' she whispered to herself.

The idea of Chuzzle being afraid gave Jilly new confidence. She climbed a little quicker. Rain ran down her face, dripping off her nose and chin. She dried her hands on her hoodie, then climbed some more.

'It's not fair to leave me out,' whined Chuzzle, 'How come everyone else gets to go to Skiddleyphet except for me? I'm a friendly fellow. I mean no harm.'

'Because you lie and cheat and pretend to be someone you're not,' called Jilly, more boldly than before. The Nine were climbing higher and higher, and the light from their storm-lanterns swished over them.

'You're not exactly perfect yourself,' said Chuzzle.

Jilly ignored the insult. She kept going. It was hard work. Her hands were sore. Her legs ached. She stopped for a moment to rest and stretch.

'I said you're not exactly perfect yourself,' Chuzzle repeated.

This time Jilly answered, 'I never said I was, but at least I'm not planning to wreck other people's lives.'

Chuzzle hooked one knee into a gap between the Stormflower and the beanstalks. He hung upside-down and flung his arms out, squinting into the dark clouds above. He cried, 'That's it. They've all gone. They've abandoned you, Jilly.'

'No, they haven't,' she said, but she was beginning to feel very alone. She stammered, 'Th . . . they wouldn't.'

'They only called you from the mountain ledge because you had the seed. They don't need you anymore.'

'Chuzzle's right,' Jilly thought, 'no one's calling me now.'

'Scruffy little Jacky-Snacky lied to you. Did he not say, "Come see The Amazing?" but he never told you what or where, because there is no Amazing.'

Jilly thought, 'Chuzzle's right again. There is no Amazing. Only darkness and rain and fear and aching muscles.'

'So you may as well let me by. It makes no difference to you if I pop in front of you. After one quick peek of the Gleaming Gate, I'll skim straight back down to Whey Wood. I promise.'

'I don't see why you shouldn't have just a little peek,' said Jilly.

She was thinking, 'They did leave me. I'm so tired of climbing for nothing. I could stop and go home.'

'Griddling greatnesses, you've seen sense at last. I knew all along you'd understand.'

Jilly felt so exhausted, the thought of Kerry's delicious food and a warm, comfortable bed was tempting. She gripped the stalk firmly and twisted her body, trying to be helpful by moving out of Chuzzle's way. 'If I hold on like this, and hang back, you can pass me . . .'

Without warning, darkness descended. Thick clouds wrapped Jilly and Chuzzle in pitch blackness. No lantern light from The Nine shone through. The rain stopped, though the droplets from the clouds soaked through Jilly's clothes. Jilly shivered. She could not stop her teeth chattering. She pressed her face into the shoot of the Stormflower and waited for Chuzzle to pass over. 'Do not stop,' came the quiet voice of Stegalegs. 'I have to . . .' Jilly trembled.

'Do not fear.'

'I am not afraid, but I am tired . . .' Jilly whispered.

'Strength is within you.'

'But I am weak.'

'Be strong as the Beanstalk is strong.'

'But I want to give up.'

'Be faithful as the Beanstalk is faithful.'

Jilly bit her lip and decided, 'I will be strong and faithful.' She had spoken out loud.

Suddenly, Chuzzle sneezed so violently the Stormflower shook. A shower of water droplets fell from the leaves to the earth, sending glittering sparkles through the pitch darkness. Jilly reached up with one hand, feeling for a good grip, but her hand was too small to wrap around the stem.

'I've got you!' cried Jackal-Yackle Snickle-Snackle, leaning down from above and snatching her hand in his, 'Come quickly, Jilly, you can do this.'

With a stupendous effort, Jilly climbed again.

Chuzzle cried, 'Where are you going now? Hey, Jilly, you

promised to let me pass.' He wiped snot from his nose with his sleeve. His soggy green hair hung limp over his shoulders. 'I'm warning you,' Chuzzle whined, then his voice became menacing, 'They will cast you off before the final lightning strikes.'

Jilly gripped Jackal-Yackle Snickle-Snackle's hand. She climbed the final metre.

Daylight burst upon her. The bright light made Jilly blink and gasp. She found herself on firm ground above the dark cloud. The Nine were sitting in long, lush grass, sharing food from Lumber's pan. Mr Jurado, with his back against a rock, stroked his beard and sipped herbal tea from a tin mug. Jilly stumbled towards them, looking from one to the other in disbelief.

'Hooray for Jilly Jonah of Whey House!' cried Felicity-Blue. She high-fived Zoa, who high-fived each of the others in turn.

Jackal-Yackle Snickle-Snackle welcomed Jilly with an exaggerated bow, throwing back his hands with a swirl, and lowering his nose until it almost touched the ground. He lifted his head and gestured for Jilly to turn around. Their eyes met. Jackal-Yackle Snickle-Snackle's eyes shone with pride, and Jilly knew he had seen The Amazing.

Jilly followed the boy's gaze. She turned to see the magnificent head of the Stormflower had opened.

The flowerhead was bigger than Whey House, wider than Cockroach Cave, and crowned with a million golden petals as bright as any sun. The petals surrounded a dome of bronze-coloured seeds, alive with shimmering butterflies settling, stunning goldfinches feasting, and bumblebees buzzing. Ladybirds and shield-bugs landed upon it. Spiders and greenfly, wasps and hoverflies, insects, moths, birds and bugs too numerous to mention, settled upon the Stormflower.

The Nine stared, their eyes shining, their mouths wide open. Jackal-Yackle Snickle-Snackle said, 'More beautiful than the Stormflower are the flowers of Skiddleyphet.'

Mr Jurado said, 'More wonderful than all the birds and butterflies upon the Stormflower are the beasts of Skiddleyphet.'

Zoa said, 'More precious than the golden petals of the

Stormflower are the people of Skiddleyphet.'

Jilly held her breath until she could hold it no longer. She fell to her knees and cried, 'It is real. I see the Amazing.'

*

The rope around Jilly's waist broke. It fell to the ground and lay still as a snake in the grass.

15
The Fall of Chuzzle

Zoa screamed, 'Look out!'

Chuzzle's curly green hair appeared above the cloud, then his azure eyes, wrinkled nose and wide, thin mouth. He grinned, 'Goody, goody, everybody's here. I do love a party.'

Mr Jurado rose to his feet. 'Help me, Felicity-Blue,' he said, softly. Felicity-Blue moved to stand beside the ancient man. Mr Jurado took her arm and together they walked towards Chuzzle. He said, 'The Stormflower stands strong, even when the greedy Chuzzle climbs it.'

Chuzzle hauled himself out of the cloud and onto the green land. He brushed the dust off his clothes. 'Phew, what a climb,' he puffed. He shielded his eyes, 'Someone switch off the light, will you? I can hardly see a dicky bird.'

Zoa linked arms with those around her. Together they hummed the Song of Courage.

Chuzzle covered his ears, 'Be quiet! Stop that nasty noise. I command you to stop.'

Mr Jurado shuffled towards Chuzzle until they were face to face.

'Not so close,' warned Felicity-Blue, 'Don't get his poisonous breath on you.'

Mr Jurado shuffled closer until his nose was almost touching Chuzzle's. His eyes narrowed, 'How did you do it?'

Chuzzle winked at Jilly, 'Me do what? Don't point your finger at me, old man. Blame her.'

'What did you give to Jilly?'

Straightaway Jilly knew what they were talking about. She felt around her waist. 'I must have lost your rope. I'm so sorry, Chuzzle. I did try to give it back to you but . . .'

Chuzzle's eyes glanced down by Jilly's feet. Jilly followed where he looked. 'There it is!' Jilly cried. She was about to pick up the rope when a quiet voice broke in,

'Do not touch.'

The gigantic silhouette of Stegalegs appeared across a mighty wall of mist which rose like a screen over the land. Stegalegs' hairy back seemed to burn in a halo of colours around the shadow[2]. Zoa, Minto and Shtomp, Archer, Joiner and Lumber stopped humming.

Jilly turned away from the shadow towards the light. The Gleaming Gate had opened. The body of the real Stegalegs filled the space between the gate posts. His eight legs and hairy back flared like fire. His eight dark, beady eyes stared, unblinking. When he spoke, he did not move his mouth.

'Do not touch the rope.'

Jilly heard Stegalegs but she didn't understand why she had to obey him. She longed to pick up the rope and return it to Chuzzle. Her hand twitched.

Chuzzle frowned, 'Don't listen to that silly old spider, Jilly. It is only a bit of old rope. Nothing special. Pass it here and you'll be rid of me.' Chuzzle stepped towards the rope. Mr Jurado moved in front of him to block him.

'Come on, you guys,' implored Chuzzle, 'I only want to hang out with you. You know me, I'm your friend. I even taught you to whistle, didn't I, Jilly?'

The Nine looked at each other with shocked expressions.

---

2 How do shadows of people appear on a cloud?

Jilly is seeing a **Brocken spectre**. This is also known as a **Brocken bow** or a **mountain spectre**

Imagine you are standing on a mountain top. The sun is setting behind you. In the distance you can see fog or low cloud. The sun is behind you, so your body casts a gigantic shadow onto the fog. This shadow is called a Brocken spectre. Sometimes the shadow is surrounded by a coloured halo. This happens when water droplets in the clouds make the sunlight refract (totally change direction) which backscatters the sunlight. (Yes, like a rainbow!)

Three facts about the Brocken spectre

The Brocken is a peak in the Harz Mountains in Germany where it is often foggy.

A spectre is another name for a ghost or spooky being.

The first person to describe a Brocken spectre was called Johann Silberschlag (1718).

Zoa gasped, 'You let him teach you how to whistle?'

Jilly said, 'Why not? Don't be so dramatic. He's more harmless than you think. He's not so bad when you get to know him properly.'

Chuzzle nodded enthusiastically, 'You heard the girl - I'm not so bad.'

'Leave,' commanded Mr Jurado, 'before the Stormflower dies.'

In a snap, Chuzzle's voice changed from charming to furious, 'Be like that, I'll get the rope myself!' He sidestepped Mr Jurado and dived for the rope.

In a split second, Stegalegs stood over the rope. Chuzzle sprawled over the grass, with his hand stretching for the rope. His fingertips wriggled and stretched but he could not quite reach.

Jilly argued, 'Why are you being so mean to Chuzzle? What's so great about that old rope? Why can't we just give it to him?'

'Because it is a tracker,' explained Jackal-Yackle Snickle-Snackle, 'and it smells of Chuzzle.'

'Ugh!' said Jilly, rubbing her waist where the rope had been.

Jackal-Yackle Snickle-Snackle continued, 'A tracker and a controller. With this rope Chuzzle tried to control your actions.'

'Is that why I couldn't pull the net out of the bridge?' cried Jilly, 'But I had the Seed of the Stormflower which Chuzzle couldn't touch. Chuzzle needed me to plant it, so why did he even try to stop me going with you?'

Jackal-Yackle Snickle-Snackle shook his head, 'I don't know.'

Chuzzle sneered, 'I was stalling you. I wanted you to be my friend, not theirs. If you hadn't chased them up the cliff, we could have gone together, just you and me. We could have planted the seed without them. We could have climbed the Stormflower together. Beat the lot of them through that gate. We would have ruled Skiddleyphet together.'

Jilly turned on Chuzzle and yelled, 'The whole time you were tracking me?'

'Hush, Jilly,' said Mr Jurado.

'No, I won't hush. I'm disgusted with him.'

Stegalegs stared at Chuzzle with his searching, black eyes. Chuzzle tried to stare back but he couldn't keep eye contact. He backed away, cowering like a frightened dog, feeling behind himself for the shoot of the Stormflower, trying not to fall into the space where the shoot pushed through the cloud. His fingertips touched a leaf. He used the leaf to guide his hand closer and closer to the stem of the Stormflower. Quick as a flash, he reached out and grabbed the stem.

Turning, he leapt onto it, wrapped his legs and arms around, and yelled, 'They're not going to let you into Skiddleyphet, Jilly. They're going to force you to go home after all you've done for them.' Chuzzle slid down the stem until only his curly green hair showed above the cloud, 'Think about it, Jilly, I'll be waiting here for you!'

Jilly turned to The Nine, 'Is that true?'

'Does Chuzzle ever tell the truth?' asked Mr Jurado quietly.

Jackal-Yackle Snickle-Snackle said, 'We will never force you to do anything. You always have a choice, Jilly Jonah. Come with us or return to your family. We can't force you, but we strongly advise you to go home.'

Jilly's eyes filled with tears, 'Are you saying you don't want me? You tricked me, Jackal-Yackle Snickle-Snackle. I trusted you, Zoa, and you tricked me. I gave away my dream for you. I thought you were my friends forever.'

The Nine, led by Felicity-Blue softly sang,
'Oh, you don't know what you're doing here yet
You cannot catch a Fogling in a net
But you carried all we need
In a dark and tiny seed
And brought us to the Land of Skiddleyphet.'

Jilly looked from Jackal-Yackle Snickle-Snackle, to Chuzzle and back again, 'Can't I just nip through the Gleaming Gate for a super quick peep?'

Mr Jurado shook his head, ever so slightly, 'That is not a

good plan.'

Jackal-Yackle Snickle-Snackle stepped forward, 'You need to say goodbye.'

'I don't get it. Why can't I do what I want when I want?'

Zoa called out, 'When you abandoned your dream for us you stopped thinking about yourself. That was unselfish. Unselfish people are strong. When you listened to Stegalegs, you were faithful.'

Mr Jurado said, 'Strong, faithful, unselfish.'

'Like the beanstalks,' said Archer.

'And the Stormflower,' added Lumber.

Felicity-Blue cried, 'We will always love you!'

Shtomp and Minto stepped forward, 'We have a gift for you.'

'A gift?' Jilly looked to see what they were offering but their hands were empty.

Lumber said, 'You will know it when you see it.'

Joiner added, 'When the Gleaming Gate finally closes, the last lightning will strike. Then the Stormflower will shake and die.'

Archer said, 'The seeds will shower our thanks upon you.'

'But I'd rather go with you than have any gift.'

Jackal-Yackle Snickle-Snackle said, 'When the last lightning flashes we will enter Skiddleyphet. There is no way back for us. Only Stegalegs is free to move between worlds.'

'You said his name.'

'I did. Thanks to you, Jilly, I am no longer afraid.'

The others echoed, 'We are not afraid of Stegalegs.'

The boy sat down and pulled the strings on his shoes. He kicked them off and wriggled his toes. 'Remember when you didn't want to put these on? I didn't blame you. They're worn out, snapped and smelly. But you were kind to me. You walked in my shoes while you carried the Seed of the Stormflower. That means so much to me.'

Jilly said, 'I'm going to stay with you forever and ever. I don't want to lose you, any of you.' She looked from one to the other of the Nine.

Mr Jurado stroked his beard, 'Enough talk. If you really want to come with us after our warning, then you may. If you do this, you can never go home.'

Stegalegs stepped back from the rope, 'Choose.'

*

Chuzzle's face popped up from the cloud. 'I told you they were tricking you. You and I make a great team. We could have ruled the world. You keep the rope, Jilly. It's my gift.'

Jilly ripped her mum's scarlet scarf from around her hair. Using the scarf to protect her hand, she dipped down, grabbed the rope with the scarf, and threw both the scarf and the rope into the gap in the clouds. The ragged rope flickered, and the scarlet scarf fluttered down beside the stalk of the Stormflower.

'My rope!' cried Chuzzle from somewhere inside the dark cloud. He reached for his rope and let go, 'Aaargh!'

All was quiet.

Jilly fell to her knees beside the hole and peered over. The leaves that Chuzzle had trodden on were snapped and bruised.

'I can't see Chuzzle,' she said, a little sadly.

'Chuzzle is fallen,' said Stegalegs.

16
What the Fogling Did

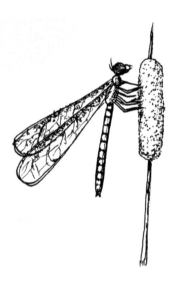

The morning sun turned Spinning River orange. Mist drifted through the bulrushes. Gentle waves lapped the riverbank. A kingfisher with a small fish in its beak, landed on a twig.

Jilly dragged her fingers through her hair, tugging at the knots. She muttered, 'Hmm, I've lost something or someone, but I can't think what it is.' Jilly pulled back the ivy that hung over the mouth of the cave and peered in. 'Nope, nothing and no one,' she sighed. She turned to gaze up at the steep cliff on far side of the river, where she had climbed with The Nine. Swirling cloud obscured her view of the top. She heard a familiar sound of bluebells and music and laughter.

'Foglings!' cried Jilly. She rushed down to the water's edge. And there they were, hundreds of grey babies, bumping fists, shaking hands, and waving goodbye to each other. One of them tumbled over to Jilly.

Fogling: You're a bit late if you've come to play.
Jilly said, 'I didn't come to play.'
Fogling: It's rude to talk with your mouth open.
Jilly (thinking): I forgot.
Fogling: That's better. We can understand your thoughts, but not your words.
Jilly: I had a net but—

Fogling: This one?

Many of the Foglings zoomed away in all directions to homes all over the world, but a few curious ones gathered round Jilly. Two Foglings in romper-suits somersaulted over the net. Another tossed a small frog into the net, but the frog jumped out and disappeared into the river. Jilly watched it swim down, down, down.

Jilly squealed, 'How did you find my net? I threw it over the edge of Silk Falls never to be seen again.'

Fogling: Talking! When you speak you confuse us.
Jilly: Where did you find it?
Fogling: In a whirlpool by Silk Falls.
Jilly: I brought it to catch a Fogling.
Fogling: No one can catch a Fogling.
Fogling: You can't catch a Fogling in a net.
Fogling: You can't catch a Fogling ever.
Jilly: It was only for fun, like catching butterflies.
Fogling: Catching is no fun for butterflies. Catching is no fun for Foglings.
Fogling: Come away home, before the sun rises. No . . . time.

All the Foglings vanished. The last two dropped the net and whizzed away, one to the north and the other to the south, leaving fluffy trails in the mist.

Jilly watched the trails evaporate, then thought, 'My net!' and went to pick it up. She swiped it through the air a couple of times, 'I guess I'm going to have to hang around until tomorrow if I'm going to catch a Fogling.' She burst into a loud song, 'You don't know what you're doing here yet, you cannot catch a Fogling in a net . . .' She faced the square head of the net and said, 'I will catch a Fogling if it's the last thing I do!'

Something (or someone) tapped Jilly on the shoulder. She swung round to see Crisp, her baby brother. His hands and face were fuzzy as a broken screen.

Fogling (Crisp): Hurry, I must leave.
Jilly: Crisp, how did you get here? Don't go - you're fading.
Fogling: Pass me the net and hold on.

Jilly clutched the net to her body, 'No, it's mine! Go home by yourself, I've got unfinished business. I'll see you tomorrow.'
Crisp fizzled out, then came back into view. He hovered around Jilly's head. She ducked. He rolled down her shoulder. She pushed him off. He tumbled close to the head of the net. Jilly swiped at him. He dived. She missed. She whipped the net over. It was upside-down, then the right way up. Crisp was inside.
'Got you!' cried Jilly. She screamed as her feet left the ground. She gripped the handle of the net, crying, 'I'm slipping. I'm going to fall.' Crisp rested in the head of the net. His feet dangled over the edge as he communicated with his big sister.

Crisp: It's okay, you are safe. You cannot fall.
Jilly: It's . . . a little . . . easier . . . now.
Crisp: You caught me.
Jilly: I did?
Crisp: You caught a Fogling in a net.
Jilly: I did?
Crisp: But the sun is rising fast. Hold tight.

Crisp and Jilly flew faster than a spitfire over Spinning River, with Crisp in the net and Jilly holding on for all she was worth, her curly hair blowing wildly, and her feet flying out behind. They whizzed under waterfalls, along Piper's Path beside Hamelin Lake, through the tunnel of brambles, into the clearing where Chuzzle had been, past the mulberry bush where Nasuto had been, over the muddy puddle that soaked Barker, past the sickly lime tree, over the mosquito-infested marsh behind the rickety shed and - whooomph - the net fell to the ground.
'Ouch!' Jilly cried, rubbing her backside. She jumped up quickly and brushed herself off. She looked around for Crisp,

but he was nowhere to be seen.

Jilly was stunned to see twelve giant sunflowers in full bloom. Each head of golden petals was higher than the shed, and each was supported by a strong stalk. And at the centre of each head a dome of fresh seeds buzzed with bees, butterflies and blue tits.

On the far side of the lawn, Whey House loomed large. Over the front door hung masses of purple wisteria flowers like bunches of grapes on a twisted vine. The door opened. Jilly's mum, Gemma, popped her head out.

'Oh, there you are, Jilly,' Gemma waved, 'Kerry's been looking all over for you. She wants you to help fetch in the washing. It got soaked yesterday, what with all that rain, and then that ferocious storm. She ended up leaving it out all night. Breakfast's in five. I'll just nip upstairs to sort the baby.' Gemma slammed the warped front door and the whole house rattled.

The back door opened. Kerry came outside carrying an empty wash-basket. She looked up at the sky and smiled, 'Sunshine and a light breeze after a storm. Don't you just love it? Perfect drying weather.' She crossed the lawn to feel the laundry on the line. 'These are ready to bring in at last,' she called to Jilly, 'Your dad had to come home early because of the storm. He saw lightning hit the oak tree. It caught fire! We were about to call the fire brigade but, thankfully, the rain put the fire out just in time. The whole place could have gone up in flames. I told you those woods are dangerous.'

Jilly said nothing. She gazed up at the sunflowers. She touched one, then another. Their leaves were thick, and their stalks were hairy. Kerry had put down the wash-basket and was heading Jilly's way.

'I was about to ask you to help me, but just look at the state of you! Your hoodie's absolutely filthy. What've you been doing? Rolling in a cow pat? You're not going near my washing. Pooh! You absolutely stink of dung. Your poor mum has quite enough to do without having to scrub stains out of your clothes. And your hair! You're scruffier than a labradoodle in a lake. Tie it up out of your eyes or you'll be seeing things that aren't there.'

'I did tie it up,' Jilly said, patting her hair and wondering what was missing from it.

'Don't lie to me, young lady, I wasn't born yesterday,' tutted Kerry through the gap in her middle tooth. Spotting the net on the ground, she added, 'What's more, you've been in the shed. If I told you once, I told you a million times, that shed is dangerous.'

'What?' said Jilly, because she wasn't listening.

'I said, the shed is dangerous. Now tell me the full truth, where have you been?'

'With Stegalegs.'

'Stega-who? Anyone would think you've been all the way to Skiddleyphet the way you're talking.'

Jilly's eyes opened wide, 'You've heard of Skiddleyphet?'

'Now there's a story I could tell you,' winked Kerry and turned to go.

Bang! A deafening thunderclap. At the same time, a blinding flash flooded the sky. Kerry swung round, 'Did you see that?'

'Zero,' cried Jilly, 'That's the last lightning!' Jilly and Kerry looked up to see, not stormy clouds, but clear blue sky. And against the sky a tiny red speck drifting slowly down towards them.

'I think it's a ribbon,' said Kerry as it fell closer.

'Or a snake,' grinned Jilly. It landed softly at Jilly's feet.

Kerry said, 'I don't believe my eyes. That's your mum's best silk scarf!'

'Um, yeah, maybe it is,' Jilly shrugged, 'I, um, lost it.' She hugged the scarf to herself and then, waving it as hard as she could she cried, 'Thank you, Jackal-Yackle Snickle-Snackle!'

'Thank who?'

'Jackal-Yackle Snickle-Snackle. He's the first of the Nine.'

'And Jilly makes ten,' joked Kerry, because she didn't understand.

'They'll be walking through the Gleaming Gate,' smiled Jilly, imagining Mr Jurado leaning on Felicity-Blue, with Zoa and the rest of The Nine dancing around.

'Now I know you're talking Skiddley-Diddley,' laughed Kerry, 'Stega-pegs, lightning under blue sky, gates to goodness-knows-where. Whatever next - invisible cats? Spying cows? You're a daft one, you are. Oh, my word, what's that?'

Hundreds and thousands of Stormflower seeds rained from the sky. 'Yes!' yelled Jilly, and she danced, whirling round and round with open arms, 'My friends are thanking me.'

The seeds pitter-pattered over the ground. Some fell among the purple thistles, some between the crazy paving stones, and others landed on hard soil. A flock of sparrows appeared from of Whey Wood. Up-down-up-down-up-down went their little brown heads, peck, peck, peck, gobbling as many seeds as they possibly could.

Some seeds sunk into softer soil, snuggling down - until next year.

One single, solitary seed slipped into the breast pocket of Jilly's hoodie.

*

'Breakfast!' called Gemma from an open window. She held baby Crisp in her arms.

Kerry abandoned the wash-basket, 'Quick, Jilly, give me that scarf. I'll take it to the dry cleaner's, so your poor mum won't ever have to find out where it's been. Come on Jilly, let's go inside and get you cleaned up.'

Jilly kicked off her trainers by the back door. She paused to watch a pretty garden spider spinning a web in the wisteria. She whispered into the web, 'Your big brother at the Gleaming Gate.'

Something twitched inside Jilly's hoodie pocket. She felt it move. She peered in and pulled out a small, brown seed. She held the seed up against the morning sun, 'Oh no you don't!' she cried. With all her might Jilly Jonah of Whey House tossed the seed across the lawn.

Who knows where the Seed of the Stormflower

fell?

The End

List of Characters

Jilly Jonah
Stegalegs

Chuzzle
Barker
Nasuto – named after the dinosaur,
Nasutoceratops Titusi

Jackal-Yackle Snickle-Snackle
Mr Jurado
Zoa
Felicity-Blue
Archer, Lumber and Joiner – they call
themselves triplets
Minto and Shtomp – the Fire-brothers

Lots of Foglings – grey babies who
play in the mist
Crisp – Jilly's baby brother, who is
also a Fogling
Kerry Muckle – a woman who lives
with the Jonah family
Gemma Jonah – Jilly's mum
And Jilly's dad – he is a dentist who likes cycling

Grow Your Own Stormflower

You will need:
Sunflower seeds – there are many varieties. I like "Russian Giant." Depending on the variety they take 80 to 120 days to grow.

Dwarf varieties grow up to your knees, but giant varieties grow halfway up a house!

Multi-purpose compost – or some good earth from your garden.

A big pot, but any pots will do. Or better still, plant straight into your garden soil, by a wall or fence is best. Sunflowers don't like being moved very much, so if you plant them in a pot they should stay in a pot.

When?

When you plant them depends on where you live – plant them outside after the last frost has passed. Sunflowers enjoy temperatures from 64 - 91°F (18–33°C).

How?

Seeds need water: Wrap seeds in a damp paper towel. Place in a plastic bag or an airtight container. Keep in a warm room. After 2 days they should burst open. Tiny shoots appear. At last they are ready to be planted outside.

Seeds need sunshine: Choose a sunny patch in your garden or on your balcony.

Seeds need compost: Sunflowers gobble goodness from the soil. Before planting, add some compost to the soil.

Now What?

Sow: Plant your sprouting seeds 2.5cm deep and 15cm apart. Be patient. Just like you, sunflowers need plenty of time to grow up

Protect: Birds and squirrels eat seeds, so maybe cover the ground with netting until the shoots are strong. As they grow you can gently tie them to a bamboo cane, to help them stand strong in any weather.

Care: Water regularly but not too much. Don't drown them!

Harvest: The flowers bloom for a month or two. Birds and insects love the seeds, so enjoy watching them. Cover some flowerheads with paper bags to save a few seeds for planting next year. When the heads have fully dried out, cut them off and keep in a shed or other dry place.

Well done, you did it!

When life is tough it can feel like you are in a dark place.

You might feel as if you have been buried,

but maybe you have been planted.

Seeds are buried in a dark place.

After many months a seed sends a tiny shoot up into the light.

Sun warms, rain waters. The shoot pushes up through the dark soil.

It grows taller and stronger every day.

In time it produces leaves, then fruit and flowers.

When life feels dark, the light is out there.

Be patient. Have hope. Grow.